FIREFLIES

A NOVEL

BY DAVID MENON

David was born in Derby, England in 1961. He's lived all over the UK but now divides his time between Paris and the northwest of England. In 2009 he left a long career in the airline industry to concentrate on his writing. He also teaches English to foreign students, mainly Russians, and is an activist for the Labour party. He's an avid fan of the American poet and singer Stevie Nicks who he calls the 'voice of my inner being', he loves red wine, gin and tonic, travelling and Indian food.

'Fireflies' is the second of his Detective Jeff Barton series of books. 'Sorcerer' was the first and he's now working on the third which will be called 'Storms'.

For Maddie or, as I now call him, Mr. Orlov … for Uncle Malcolm and Aunty Lesley with whom I have to make up so much time … and for anyone who can find no easy way in the drama of the moment.

FIREFLIES PROLOGUE

The bride and groom checked into the wedding suite at the Manchester Hilton hotel and the groom carried the bride over the threshold. The room had been a surprise present from the groom's parents and they'd even ordered a bottle of champagne which duly arrived a few minutes after the happy couple did. They'd already drunk their own body weight of the stuff all day but as this was a day that neither of them intended to ever repeat, they considered it an obligation to pop the cork and dive right in.

They jumped on the bed and cradled each other in their arms whilst they sipped more of one the greatest French exports. In a little over twenty-four hours they'd be sipping cocktails on the balcony of their hotel room on the island of Phuket in Thailand where they'd be staying for a week before flying on to Melbourne in Australia to stay with the bride's Aunt and Uncle. They were looking forward to their honeymoon. Why wouldn't they be? Apart from the adventure of being in faraway lands a honeymoon was a way for the couple to extend the joy of their wedding day but without the company of all the guests. Their flight left Manchester airport at just before ten-thirty in the morning with a change at Abu Dhabi. They set their alarm and phoned down to reception to ask for a wake-up call. They'd be shattered when they got on that plane but it would be the best shattered feeling they'd ever experience.

The room at the Hilton had a floor to ceiling window that offered the most incredible view of their home city that either of them had ever seen. They could see the lights stretching all the way up to Rochdale and Bolton in the north and Salford to the west. They'd bought a house in Salford but they wouldn't be able to move in for a month so when they came back from honeymoon they'd be staying with the bride's parents for a couple of weeks until the builders had finished their work. Everything about the joy of living together as a couple bound by love was waiting there in front of them. It was theirs to take the necessary steps to reach their own particular bliss.

The groom wasn't a heavy smoker but he did like the odd one or two. He hadn't had one since they'd been halfway through the dancing at the reception so whilst the bride did what she wanted to do to prepare for her wedding night, the groom nipped outside for a fag. They'd already had sex in a back room of the restaurant in Alderley Edge where they'd held the reception. The groom had still been in his tails and the bride was of course in her wedding dress. She asked him to wear his top hat whilst they did it and it fell right off just at the appropriate moment.

When the groom got back up to the suite the door was slightly open. He pushed it wider and called out his wife's name but the fact was he was already a widower. He walked round to the bedroom and there she was lying on the bed, still in her dress but with blood pouring out of the many stab wounds to her neck, face, and other parts of her body. The attack would later be described as 'frenzied'. Her eyes were open but her soul had left her husband behind. He shrieked with terror and pain. The dreams of two people who'd been so in love had been shattered in such a brutal and sick way. Who would want to do something like this? He slid down the wall and crashed onto the floor. His heart was broken and so was his soul. He began to weep. He didn't think he'd ever be able to stop.

FIREFLIES ONE

Alicia Zolkiewicz had recently been joined by her husband Stefan in a life they were building together in England. They came from Gdansk on the northern edge of Poland and though it meant leaving their two daughters to be cared for by Stefan's parents it was worth it. Even accounting for the cost of the two-day coach journey each way that they made whenever they could amass enough hours in their respective jobs to get a full week off to go home and see their kids, and even though it meant they had to stay in the tiniest of bedsits in a nevertheless not too bad area of Stockport, it was all better than they could get at home. And they weren't alone. They were surrounded by every nationality under the sun in a giant melting pot of people wanting to gain more than their own home countries could offer. Alicia and Stefan spent little money. They lived frugally. They were better off than some of their compatriots where either the wife or the husband had to come to England on their own. They missed their daughters every minute of every day but moving to England was worth it when they could provide them with so much more than if they'd stayed to work in Poland. The British are always complaining but they really don't know how well off they are.

Stefan was now a bus driver and worked out of the main depot in Stockport's Mersey square. He was beginning to really enjoy his work. He liked being with people all day and it was an excellent way for him to continually improve his conversation skills. It was the same for Alicia and her job at the hotel. She was employed as a waitress in the restaurant where all meals, breakfast, lunch, and dinner were served on a 'buffet' style basis and apart from putting the food out and replenishing it when necessary, her other main function was to serve drinks from the bar. Today she was on the early shift starting at six and she walked swiftly in the darkness the half a mile from their flat to the Mayfair hotel which was situated on the main road leading out of the city towards the town of Marple in the Peak District. She got there with ten minutes to spare and decided to sneak out the back where the rubbish bins are for a cigarette. She was about to light up when she saw something she certainly hadn't expected to see on this average Sunday morning and the shock led to her giving out a blood curdling scream.

Detective Superintendent Jeff Barton pulled up outside the Mayfair hotel feeling very bleary eyed. He hadn't counted on being woken up at stupid o'clock on a rare Sunday morning when he could lie in bed and think about nothing except catching up on sleep. He was greeted by his partner in crime, Detective Sergeant Rebecca Stockton who'd arrived just a few minutes before.

'Sorry to get you up so early on a Sunday, sir' said Rebecca.

'It's not like it's the first time, Becky' answered Jeff.

'What have you done with Toby?'

'He's staying over with his Chinese grandparents this weekend which was lucky' Jeff explained. 'I spoke to him a few minutes ago and he was tucking into a soup with noodles, mushrooms, and prawns and his grandfather is teaching him Mandarin. I love it that he gets an insight into his mother's culture. It means he holds onto something of her'.

'What would you have done if he wasn't with his grandparents?'

That was a tough question for Jeff. He'd been wondering a lot lately about what to do long-term about Toby's childcare. He knew that his brother Lewis and his partner Seamus didn't mind at all sharing Toby. They adored him and Toby adored them too. But that didn't help Jeff feeling bad about it. Lewis and Seamus have got their own life to live. They shouldn't have to think about Lewis's nephew before they planned even a weekend away.

'Our Lewis and his partner Seamus are so good to us and then I can sometimes rely on Pam next door' said Jeff. 'Her two are Toby's best mates'.

'Toby doesn't seem unhappy about his lot at the moment' said Rebecca. 'He seems like a really well adjusted kid despite everything'.

'No I know' said Jeff. 'He is and I'm grateful for that. But I worry about the lack of long-term stability for him'.

'Jeff, kids adjust a lot better than their parents give them credit for' said Rebecca. 'And he gets that stability from you'.

'I know that too' said Jeff.

'Have you thought about getting a nanny?'

'Well funnily enough Lewis and Seamus have got a mate who's just qualified as a nanny and he wants a position where he lives in'.

'Sounds ideal'.

'Yeah but I don't know'.

'Jeff, don't tell me you don't want him to have a male nanny?'

'Don't be ridiculous, you know me and I've got no qualms on that score at all'.

'So what's the problem?'

'Well it's just that Toby is surrounded by dudes, you know. Me, Lewis, Seamus. He doesn't have any regular women in his life. A bit like his father'.

Rebecca smiled. 'Well he's got his teacher at school, his Chinese grandma and Pam your neighbour and you've got me' she said, hoping he'd see something in what she'd said although she wasn't holding her breath. 'Why don't you give this guy a trial and see how it works out? It'll give you the chance to get some of the stress off your shoulders'.

'I'll think about it' said Jeff who then looked over the u-shaped three-storey building with the gym and swimming pool attached. 'Isn't this a bit out of place? I mean, right in the middle of one of the most des res parts of Stockport? Have you ever been here?'

'Yeah, my cousin had his wedding reception here a couple of years ago' said Rebecca who noted that Jeff had once again switched off the personal talk. 'I can't say I remember much about it because the party was pretty good but I do recall thinking that it's like a lot of hotels in Britain in that it charges the earth for everything but the decorating should've been done years ago and there are creaking floors under hideous carpets everywhere'.

'And I bet they use tinned grapefruit segments at breakfast'.

'Oh that's standard in British hotels like this' said Rebecca, smiling. 'Along with the grease on everything because it's been left out too long and toast that's turned into cardboard for the same reason'.

'That's a pity because I'm starving'.

'You and me both'.

DC Oliver 'Ollie' Wright had been the first member of Jeff's team on the scene and he led them round to the back of the hotel. Ollie had become, along with Rebecca, one of Jeff's most trusted lieutenants. He was going to make sure that Ollie was promoted because he was a bloody good police officer and not one of those lick arse types who shot up the ladder even though they were incapable of finding a seagull at the coast.

The pathologist June Hawkins looked up and saw Jeff, Rebecca and Ollie lifting up the crime scene tape and putting on their white cover suits before walking over to her.

'Well it's too late for casualty that's for sure' said June in her usual deadpan way. 'Your victim is well and truly dead, darling'.

'Male or female?' asked Jeff.

'Male' June answered. 'I'd say he was in his late twenties. He didn't wear a wedding ring but then not all married men do'.

'Can you say how he died, June?' asked Jeff.

'Well his genitals have been cut off, cock and balls, the whole lot. We're searching the area to see if we can find them'. She pulled back the sheet over the body and watched all three police officers put their hands to their mouths and wretch before placing it back. 'He'd have died from the bleeding if not the pain and shock of it actually happening'.

'So you think he may have been still alive when the mutilation took place?' asked Ollie.

'Well he could've been, yes' said June. 'There are no signs of restraint. No rope marks around his wrists or ankles for example. Now he wouldn't have volunteered willingly for this particular service so I speculate that he was probably drugged. I'll know for sure one way or the other when I get him back to the lab for tests'.

'Somebody must've really hated him' said Ollie.

'Or kinky sex gone wrong?' Rebecca suggested.

'I think wrong is something of an understatement when he's been disembowelled' said June, smiling at her own sledgehammer wit.

'So was he a hotel guest or was he just dumped here?' Rebecca wondered.

'I take it you didn't find any ID on him, June?' Jeff asked.

'No, love, sorry' said June.

'How long would you say he's been dead, June?'

'Not long' said June. 'I'd say three or four hours at the most'.

'So he's probably not been reported as missing by anyone yet' said Ollie.

'No' said Rebecca. 'If he's only been there a short time then somebody living nearby might've seen something. They can't all have been tucked up in bed. I'll get a team down to start house to house. Then there are the hotel guests. Did any of them see anything if they happened to be gazing out of the window in the early hours'

'I'll get on to that, ma'am' said Ollie, confidently.

'We'll also need to speak to the hotel staff' said Jeff. 'I imagine some of the guests from last night will have already checked out but we can chase them up and I'll get uniforms to be at the reception desk and the exit points to stop and question everyone who leaves from now on. Who found him?'

'A young Polish girl who works as a waitress here' said Ollie. 'She's in shock as you can imagine but she's inside and she seems okay to talk'.

'The owner of the hotel is a complete cow, Jeff' said June. 'I could've punched her earlier'.

'Yes, I can verify that about Mrs. Helen Curzon, sir' said Ollie. 'She's been giving everybody a hard time. She just doesn't seem to care that this is a murder investigation'.

'So what do you think?' asked Rebecca as she and Jeff walked towards the door through to the hotel kitchen. Ollie had gone round to the reception area to co-ordinate the uniform team's efforts to take statements from the hotel guests.

'I think it looks personal to me' said Jeff. 'The killer had good reason in their mind to mutilate someone in that way. Whoever did this is making a point of some kind'

'Remind me to go on that profiling course' said Rebecca.

'Yes, I think you should' said Jeff. 'It would be useful and add to your already well honed detective skills'.

'Are you flattering me, sir?'

'Really DS Stockton' said Jeff, smiling. 'The thought never crossed my mind'.

Helen Curzon was sitting in her office next to the reception desk as if she expected all around her to dance to her tune without question. Jeff took her to be in her early fifties and she was wearing a black tailored suit of short jacket and knee length skirt. Her wavy hair was a hazel colour and swept back revealing an open face with large soft blue eyes. Her white open necked blouse looked like it came from one of the more expensive Manchester retailers and the ensemble was finished off with jewellery that could never be described as costume. Her finger nails looked false but coated in the deepest red and she had a trim figure. She clearly used much of whatever disposable income she had on her appearance. Jeff and Rebecca introduced themselves.

'And you're Mrs. Helen Curzon?' asked Rebecca.

'Yes. I'm the co-owner of the Mayfair hotel with my husband Brian'.

'Mrs. Curzon, I'm sure my colleague DC Wright has explained that we do look for your full co-operation here' said Jeff.

'And there speaks the civil servant as opposed to someone who lives in the real world of the private business owner' said Helen, her voice like ice falling on an enamel board and making a screeching sound that made everyone shudder.

'Excuse me?' said Jeff, his shackles rising.

'Detective, my husband and I have built this business up over several years and we have an enviable reputation in the higher end of the business and leisure market'.

'It still doesn't stop you offering incentives of cheap lager every Friday and Saturday night for the binge drinking crowd' Rebecca pointed out. 'I saw the posters on our way in'. She'd already had a bucket full of this odious woman.

Helen Curzon smirked as if she was speaking to a complete underling who was rather stupid. 'We meet that particular market at the weekend but it doesn't stop us from meeting a different kind of market during the week' said Helen, flatly. 'That's how private enterprise responds with flexibility'.

'Mrs. Curzon, a man has been murdered and the body left at the back of your hotel' said Jeff, sternly. 'Isn't that a matter of importance to you?'

'The only matter of importance in my life is my husband and making him happy, detective'.

'And I'm sure he very much appreciates that but back to the matter in hand if you don't mind' said Jeff.

'Oh look I'm aware of the gravity of the situation, detective' said Helen. 'Of course I am. But my hotel has 297 rooms and last night we were running at ninety percent occupancy which is no mean feat considering the current economic climate. Do you realise the implications on my business this could have?'

'I do Mrs. Curzon but with all due respect your business concerns are not at the top of my list of priorities' Jeff retorted. 'Finding a killer is. Now I presume you have a night manager?'

'Yes' said Helen as if it was causing her physical pain to co-operate. 'He went home at five because he has a dental appointment today and needed to adjust his sleep pattern. He'll be making up the hours tonight by coming in early'.

'The name of the night manager?' asked Rebecca.

'Julian Fowler. He lives over in Marple. I expect you'll require his address?'

'You expect correctly' said Jeff. 'We'll also need the names and contact details of all the staff, especially those who were on duty last night and those who started work this morning before the discovery of the body'.

Helen sighed. 'Very well'.

'Now DC Wright will be leading the team here at the hotel' said Jeff. 'I don't want to hear from him that you've been anything less than fully co-operative with our enquiries. Is that clear, Mrs. Curzon?'

She glared at him with a look that said if she could stamp on him she most certainly would. 'I don't waste my energy fighting decisions over which I have no choice'.

'I'll take that as a yes then' said Jeff. 'Do you live on the premises?'

'Heavens, no! My husband and I live in a converted stables over in Saddleworth'.

'Is he there now?'

'Yes' said Helen. 'It was my turn to do the early start. Our property is worth a considerable amount of money which we might need if this does have a downward impact on the business'.

Jeff sighed irritably. 'Does he know about the body yet?'

'No. I don't know how he'll take it. He's been worried enough about the business as it is. This is the age of the consumer and everybody wants to cut costs. Everybody wants to spend twenty pounds on a level of service that costs a hundred to deliver. One's margins are being squeezed all the time. That's why this couldn't have come at a worse time for us and furthermore I have tickets for Joan Collins and her one woman show tonight. I'm a great admirer of her. They don't make real stars with talent like her anymore'.

Talent? That's not a word Jeff would put in the same sentence as Joan Collins. He'd only ever seen her play herself.

'Like I said before Mrs. Curzon' said Jeff, testily. 'We expect your full co-operation'.

FIREFLIES TWO

Andrea Kay cursed the bloody weather. On her way into work she'd been drenched in a downpour that could've signified that November had swapped its weather for that of the current month of May.

'It's the first of June on Thursday' said Andrea as she and her friend Tina hung their coats up in the staff room. Everybody who worked at the super store liked to cover up their uniform when they were going to and from work otherwise they were accosted on the bus by elderly women who wanted to know if cat food was on special offer this week. 'And it feels like bloody winter out there'.

'It'll start rolling down the street soon if it carries on as heavily as this' Tina remarked. 'Traffic will come to a standstill, the heavens will descend on us, the world will stop spinning and all life as we know it will come to an end'.

Andrea laughed. 'You're such a fucking drama Queen. By the way, how did you get on with that fit bloke from the Paradise club on Saturday?'

'Oh, fine' said Tina who really didn't want to go into it. The fact was the whole situation had been an absolute disaster but she wasn't about to tell Andrea that. 'Anyway, nobody owns me and variety is the spice of life. You should try it'.

Andrea smiled. She and her friend were so different. Tina was outwardly confident, some would say loud and brash. She could walk into a pub anywhere on any night of the week and find a man to pull but she made damn sure she didn't get pregnant. She was only twenty-two and she didn't want a husband or even a sniff of kids until she was at least thirty which she admitted made her unusual amongst her family and some of her other friends on the estate where she came from where it wasn't unusual to be a Grandmother at the age of thirty.

'But I never see anyone I really fancy' Andrea moaned.

'There are plenty of men out there who are up for some fun. You're just too fussy'.

'And you're a tart'.

'Thank you. I model myself on how you'd be if you let yourself go. There must be bloody cobwebs up your fanny'.

'Cheeky bitch'

'Truth hurts?'

Andrea sighed. 'I don't deny it. I'm boring and I'm old before my time'.

'Don't turn into one of those women who are obsessed with finding reasons not to have sex' cried Tina. 'Because that's why so many men walk around looking so fucking miserable. All they want is a bit of legover but all their wife or girlfriend want is a baby and once that's popped out and she's a Mum then sex is confined to the past'.

'Oh go and make me a cup of tea and I'll think about whether or not I'm still talking to you'.

'Right you are, chuck' said Tina. 'By the way, doesn't the new boss start today?'

'Paula Jones?' said Andrea. 'Yes, I think she does. It was supposed to be last Monday but they put it back for some reason'.

'I still think they should've given the job to you after Phil had to retire' said Tina, ever loyal to her friend. 'Especially after you've been standing in all this time whilst we were waiting for that lot at head office to get off their collective backsides and organise themselves. It's been over three months since Phil had his heart attack'.

'Yes, well, they didn't' said Andrea. 'Have you spoken to Phil lately?'

'I went up to see him yesterday afternoon'.

'And is he okay?'

'He seems fine but he isn't if you see what I mean' Tina revealed. 'I mean, he's sleeping downstairs now. He can't manage the stairs and poor Jean is worn out, not only with the physical side of taking care of him but also with the worry of not knowing if he's going to wake up in the morning'.

'Tina?'

'What?'

'I just wanted to say thanks for, well you know, not going for the promotion yourself and giving me a clear shot at it'.

'Fat lot of good it did you'.

'I know but I'm grateful. You know I am'.

'Yes, well you were always better suited to it than me but let's hope Paula Jones is grateful for the fact that she's been parachuted in over your head'.

'I'm grateful for all the blessings in my life, thank you'.

Andrea and Tina, both momentarily shocked by the sudden appearance of a Welsh accent behind them, turned round and gave the best supermarket customer service smiles normally reserved for those daft bastards who can't find tinned tuna chunks on a shelf that's packed with them. They also hoped she hadn't overheard what they'd said.

'You must be Paula?' said Tina, offering her hand which Paula shook. 'I'm Tina Webb'.

'Hello, Tina' said Paula with the kind of smiley happy people look on her face that warned Tina that she would probably end up loathing her.

'And I'm Andrea Kay' said Andrea, also shaking hands with Paula. Andrea looked her potential new adversary up and down. She had on one of those classic two-piece dark blue and white check suits with a light blue blouse underneath. It made her look slightly on the Miss Ellie side of things when she was probably no older than Sue Ellen. Andrea knew everything about Dallas. She'd got the box set of DVDs at home and had always been madly in love with Bobby Ewing. Paula's hair was dyed blond judging by the roots and curled under just above her shoulders. She was a lady who was carrying a little more weight than she really should but Andrea thought it might be good if there was another woman in the place with hips bigger than her own.

'I feel so blessed to have been brought in to manage this prestigious branch of PriceChopper' she announced through her smiley, happy mouth. 'It has a bigger client base than any of our other stores across Greater Manchester. And Andrea, I know you've been managing it on a temporary basis these past few weeks but I can assure you that my appointment is absolutely no reflection on your ability to do the job'.

'So what is it a reflection of then?' Andrea asked.

'I'm sorry?'

'Well if, as you say, you getting this job rather than me is no reflection on my ability to do it then why did they give it to you and not me? Sorry, but you laid it wide open for me to ask you that'.

'You're absolutely entitled to your opinion, Andrea, and I for one am not ever going to deny you your feelings because they are a true reflection of your character and personality, but there's a certain amount of moving on that has to be done here if we're going to continue the success of this store'.

'Easy for you to say from where you're standing' said Andrea. 'I suppose that all the moving on has got to come from me? That's what moving on normally means. It all has to come from the one who's been wronged'.

'Well I am the manager and you're the customer services person, Andrea'.

'Actually, I'm head of fruit and vegetables'.

'Yes, sorry, I was forgetting how some get so attached to titles'.

'What happened to all the management language of we're all in this together? Isn't that what they taught us on all those tedious residential courses they sent us on? What was it called? Corporate care?'

'I designed the Corporate Care programme, Andrea'.

'So? I'm not going to take back what I've just said. It was nothing more than just a brain washing exercise to empty our minds of requesting a pay rise. You tried to tell us that shit doesn't smell if we put on an overbearing and totally meaningless smile. And let me tell you this, Paula, the success of this store is down to me and Tina here'

'Andrea, all of this will be accurately reflected in my approach to you both, I can assure you'.

'Paula?' Tina began, wanting to support her friend but not really being able to get a word in edgeways between these two warring cats until now. 'You must see how hard it is from Andrea's position?'

'I'm not responsible for however Andrea reacts to anything' Paula stated. 'That is not my problem because I'm on my own journey and Andrea is on hers'.

Tina hated that kind of psychobabble talk. 'Look, she's been working here for several years, she's been working towards this promotion for a long time now and when she finally gets in reach of it you're parachuted in because you're a favoured daughter at head office for some reason. I'm sorry, Paula, I'm sure you're very well meaning and capable and everything but some resentments can't just be instantly fixed with a painted on smile and talk of moving on and journeys. Life isn't as simple as that kind of shallow psychology because it takes no account of people's feelings'.

'But it does take the blame culture out of the workplace'.

'And also the culture of responsibility' Tina countered. 'If you don't want people to be blamed when things go wrong then nobody will ever take responsibility for anything'.

'I see' said Paula. 'Well now you've both made your positions perfectly clear why don't we draw a line under it all and start again? You never know what you'll be able to see when you close your eyes as a child and open them again as an adult'.

Tina and Andrea were both seething.

'Let me make you both a mug of herbal tea. I find that cammamile always helps in these kind of situations'.

'I'm just about to make us all a brew' said Tina. 'Of normal tea'.

'Oh, well sorry Tina but I don't drink any beverage containing caffeine since I started developing a new relationship with food that's led to me looking at my entire consumption of drink as well. You wouldn't believe how much better I feel since I started making more informed choices about what I actually put in my mouth. I'll catch you both later'.

Meeting a new Chief Superintendent isn't always fun but the omens on this particular twosome working out weren't altogether good. Newly appointed Chief Superintendent Geraldine Chambers greeted Jeff with an affable smile and a surprisingly open face. This was sometimes unusual in a chief superintendent but given the circumstances in which Geraldine Chambers had been appointed Jeff thought it a little remarkable. After all, he'd been the one to push her predecessor into confessing his corruption from years back and no matter how high they go they don't normally take well to someone who told on a colleague. She shook his hand and asked him to sit down in one of the two soft chairs she had by the window of her office. She sat in the other one and they faced each other with a view across Manchester's city centre between them. Geraldine Chambers wasn't the tallest of women and Jeff would place her in her late forties. She had light brown hair that was cut in a spiky style before tapering into her neck at the back and she wore little make-up. Her figure looked good and Jeff noticed her fingernails were cut neat and short but no polish on them. He'd been starting to notice the curves and shapes of other women again lately and wondered if what he needed was some truly adult no holds barred inhibitions free mind blowing sex with no strings attached. He'd never put himself about much before he met Lillie Mae but these were different and unexpected times. Or was it that he missed having sex with the only woman he'd ever loved? Sometimes he thought he was going mad with grief and didn't know when the agonising pain of losing Lillie Mae was ever going to end.

'I've been looking through your file, Jeff' she began.

'Oh dear' said Jeff after clearing his throat. 'That sounds ominous'.

Geraldine smiled 'Not at all. You have an excellent record and I'm pleased to have you as the senior officer on my team'.

'Well thank you, ma'am'.

'Don't mention it' said Geraldine. 'What did you expect me to say?'

Jeff felt himself blush. 'Oh, I don't know, ma'am. You know, after the events of last year'.

'Jeff, you were instrumental in exposing a corrupt officer whose actions, or lack of them, led to some very serious crimes going undetected and several teenage boys suffering horrific abuse. I don't say that everyone feels like I do but I personally wouldn't condemn you for that. I applaud you'.

Jeff smiled. 'Thank you, ma'am'.

'Now forgive me if I'm getting too personal but I understand you lost your wife not so long ago?'

'Yes, ma'am' said Jeff.

'It was tragic to lose her so young'.

'That's one word for it, ma'am'.

'It doesn't seem to have affected your work though?'

'I haven't buried myself in the job as a means of escape, ma'am'.

'I wasn't suggesting you had, Jeff. I was merely remarking on your professionalism. You've got a little boy as well I believe?'

'Yes. His name is Toby. He's ... well he's amazing'.

'I'm sure' said Geraldine, smiling. 'And helping to get you through?'

'Oh yes, ma'am. He's miles better than a therapist'.

'I have a son too although he's considerably older than Toby. He's in his first year at Durham University'.

'You must miss him?'

'Well yes I do but we haven't lived together for a few years. His father and I divorced when he was ten and my ex-husband got custody. It was then that I lost him really rather than now. Anyway, enough of my self-indulgence, I know you and your team have just picked up what may turn out to be a pretty involved case but I may have to ask you to stretch your resources a little too. The elected police commissioner wants a root and branch audit of all our operations. He wants to know if we can deliver a more effective police service more efficiently'.

Jeff rolled his eyes up. 'On the cheap'.

'Yes, that's how I initially reacted too but you never know, there might be some things we can find as potential savings that work to our advantage'.

'May I say I admire your optimism, ma'am?'

'Indeed you may' said Geraldine. 'Although I'm not sure if I admire it myself if I'm honest'.

FIREFLIES THREE

The temperature in the delivery area at the back of the supermarket was kept deliberately low. Andrea Kay walked in and immediately saw her friend Tina.

'What are you doing?' she asked rather foolishly.

'I'm about to overtake Lewis Hamilton in the Grand Prix, what does it look like I'm doing?'

Amanda gave a slight smile. 'Sorry' she said as she watched Tina deal with a fresh load of yogurts and cheeses that she was preparing to take out onto the supermarket floor.

'No, I'm the one who should be sorry' said Tina. 'I've got a bit of a headache. Did you enjoy your day off yesterday?'

'Well I didn't do much except watch This Morning, Loose Women, and the Alan Titchmarsh show'.

'Ooh stop right there because I can't take the excitement'.

'Bollocks. Can I talk to you for a minute, Teen?'

'Yeah, why, what's up?'

'I'm just worried, Tina'

'What about?'

'I'm worried that I'm going to end up in a house somewhere surrounded by cats and I won't have been kissed for a hundred years or felt a man's arms around me'.

This was where Tina had to be really honest although it was hard. Andrea was her friend and she didn't want to hurt her but what she couldn't stand was when people gave others false hope. She didn't know if Andrea was ever going to be happy and so she didn't want to go into the whole 'it'll happen for you one day because you're gorgeous and don't let anybody make you think otherwise' type of shit. Andrea scrubbed up well but she often lays open the fact that there wasn't much base material to work on. She wasn't ugly but she wasn't the prettiest either. But Tina could say that about a few of her friends and yet they'd all found men. She didn't know why Andrea had never found the right man to be with. But she did know that Andrea didn't give men a chance to be nice to her. Her defences went up as soon as any man showed any interest and she made it clear that she didn't trust any man. Well if she continued behaving that way then she would end up in a house surrounded by cats because no man is going to want to work that hard.

'You need to get out there more, Andrea' said Tina. 'Mr. Right won't come knocking on your door'.

'You have no shame'.

'You have no regular dick and that's why you get so bad tempered sometimes'.

'I do not!'

'Oh you do' said Tina. 'Usually when you've run out of batteries for that vibrator'.

'I don't have a vibrator'.

'I rest my case' said Tina. 'I'll get you one at the weekend. Do you want white or black, large or painful?'

Andrea laughed more out of embarrassment than anything else. 'I wouldn't ... well I wouldn't know how to use it'.

'You're serious?'

'Absolutely' said Andrea. 'I've led a sheltered life, Tina, you know that'.

'Well I'm not going to give you a demonstration, love! You plug it in, open your legs, stick it up there, switch it on and then imagine it's Matt Baker on the end of it'.

'I quite like Matt Baker actually' Andrea admitted. 'But he's spoken for and anyway he'd never look at the likes of me'.

Tina walked over and put her arms round her friend. 'Andrea, you're doing what a lot of women do when they've been alone for a long time. You're putting all your energy into some fantasy man who you know you'll never have. Now I wet myself over Matt Baker too but I prefer to get the most out of real life and I really want you to be happy and fulfilled'.

'Do you think I will find it?'

'I don't know, love. I hope so'.

'Thanks, Tina' said Andrea. 'You're a great listener and you don't bullshit me'.

'It's what a best friend is for. Well that and telling you how to use a vibrator'.

'What would you do with me, eh?'

'Nothing love, sorry. You know I love you to bits but I'm not licking your fanny'.

'Tina!'

'Well I'll try most things but I've never fancied the lezzy side of life'.

Andrea pulled a face. 'Me neither. All those hairs and veins'.

'I've got a gay male friend who got drunk one night and tried it with a woman. You know, Bruce the dog groomer?'

'Yeah, course I know Bruce. I've often wished he was straight'.

'We all have sweetheart but his only dive into that particular river was the first and last. He was on the phone last night for two hours. He was in a right state'.

'Why?'

'Well the girl he slept with ended up pregnant and ... '

' ... you're joking. I never knew'.

'He doesn't talk about it much, to be fair' said Tina. 'But anyway, she had a little girl who'll be ten now. I mean, would you believe it? The only time he'd ever slept with a woman and she got pregnant. I've got straight male friends who try for years with their wives to start a family and there goes Bruce sending his fish onto the right hook first time when he usually shops round the corner'.

'Does he still see his daughter?'

'He used to. But then her Mum got married to a bloke in the army and moved down to Windsor. It broke Bruce's heart. He and Chloe had got quite close, you see. They used to have loads of fun together and she was a real Daddy's girl. But her Mum put Bruce under pressure to back off when she got married and moved although she has said that when Chloe gets older and is able to understand everything then she won't stand in her way if Chloe wants to re-establish contact with him. He'd love it if she did. He really misses her and that's why every now and then, like last night, he gets really upset'.

'But it sounds like her mother didn't give him much choice if she put him under pressure to back off?'

'Well that's right she didn't. But it would've been hard to maintain regular access when Chloe is living two hundred and fifty miles away. He could've gone to court to fight it but in the end what good would that have done? It certainly wouldn't have done Chloe any good and she's the main consideration here. And he did understand that Sally, that's Chloe's Mum, had a right to be happy and start a new life with her husband who Chloe does get on with so there's no problem there. Sally sends Bruce pictures and regular updates on what Chloe's doing which believe me is a lot more than some men in his position get when they're an absentee father, gay or straight. So he is lucky in a way'.

'Poor Bruce' said Andrea who had what she could best describe as a troubled relationship with her father and was envious of a little girl called Chloe who she didn't know but who had a dedicated father like Bruce who would always be there for her no matter what. And she hated Chloe's mother for keeping Chloe's father away from her. Andrea knew how painful that felt too. 'It doesn't seem fair'.

'Well no, it isn't fair' said Tina. 'But whoever said life was fair needs a bullet through their head'.

Jeff had gathered his steadily increasing number of officers in his MIT to a briefing in the squad room. In the front of the group were DS Rebecca Stockton and DC Ollie Wright. Jeff stuck a photograph onto the clear plastic board he was stood in front of.

'We've been able to identify our disembowelled friend found at the Mayfair hotel. During a search of the hotel car park his wallet was found and we were able to match some of the pictures inside with his bank and credit cards. His name is James Clifton, aged twenty-seven and he worked for the BBC at the Media City complex at Salford Quays as a stage manager. He was originally from Preston. Over to you, DC Wright'.

Ollie cleared his throat and went and stood in the space Jeff vacated. Jeff folded his arms and perched his bottom on the edge of one of the desks.

'Clifton lived at 27 Cumberland Terrace in West Didsbury with his fiancée Sophie Cooper who is an air stewardess based at Manchester airport. She got in around seven on Sunday morning from a night return to Tenerife. She didn't think it was unusual that he wasn't home yet because she assumed he'd just passed out and slept at one of his mates like he sometimes does and was probably too pissed to even send a text. But then when he didn't turn up later in the day and none of his friends could tell her where he was she got worried. Now, he was with ten other blokes on a stag night for their friend Alan Travers. Miss Cooper said they were planning to end up at the Paradise Club at the lower end of Deansgate and across the road from Deansgate station. We've checked the CCTV and Clifton and his mates are seen going in there at 1.37. We're still going through the footage to try and see if we can spot him with anyone in particular. Meanwhile, we've been down at the hotel interviewing all the staff and we did manage to speak to everyone, including those who weren't on duty that night, and none of them claim to know anything. The two that were on duty that night didn't see or hear anything untoward. There's CCTV camera coverage of the car park but it points away from where the body was dumped. The monitors are in the office behind the reception desk. We've been through it all, sir, for that night, and absolutely nothing'.

'But surely something would've shown up on there?' asked Jeff who was rolling the name Sophie Cooper over and over in his mind. He knew her. He didn't know where from but he knew that name and it was going to drive him crazy until his memory caught up. 'We're talking about a grown man's body dumped behind those rubbish carts. How the hell could it have got there without some bastard noticing?'

'At the moment we can't tell, sir' said Ollie. 'There are no pictures of him from the public areas entering the hotel either alone or with anyone so perhaps we can say he wasn't murdered actually at the hotel. We've checked the hotel records too and are now about halfway through contacting every guest from that night. None of them so far admit to having had any connection with James Clifton and some of them are business executives living as far away as Germany and Portugal who were in town for weekend trade fairs and meetings. There was also a large wedding party in. The hotel only have a skeleton staff on during the night and on Saturday it was the night manager Julian Fowler plus a receptionist who also acted as a waitress for whoever wanted room service in the early hours. On that night the honour went to Anita Patel'.

'And that's it?' Rebecca questioned. 'Just the two of them on duty all night in a hotel that size?'

'That's it' Ollie confirmed.

'But who cooks the food if someone does want room service in the early hours?' Jeff asked.

'It's all put in the microwave by either the night manager or receptionist apparently' said Ollie

'And how did Mr Fowler and Miss Patel seem to you, Ollie?'

'Both of them seemed reluctant to talk to us but I think for different reasons, sir' said Ollie. 'Fowler is a reformed alcoholic. He's been dry now for ten years and doesn't seem to take much interest in anything other than not thinking about alcohol. As for Miss Patel, she shares a basement flat in the hotel with four other members of staff who are also all from India or Bangladesh. The gym and swimming pool are managed separately to the hotel but our interviews there have drawn a blank too in terms of James Clifton. We did get some of the hotel staff to open up eventually and they told us that they all get paid weekly, cash in hand, but if not enough cash has been taken across reception and the bar and the restaurant, if most customers have paid their bill by card in other words, then nobody gets paid and the wages are held over till the next week'.

'What?' said Rebecca. 'The rotten bastards. Is that legal?'

'Well even if it is legal it's not moral' said Jeff. 'But it doesn't surprise me given the attitude we got from Helen Curzon'.

'And they pay just on the minimum wage' Ollie went on. 'Not a penny more and the staff are all on zero hours contracts. The Curzon's have cut everything in the hotel down to the bone. The staff are told that if a guest complains about something not working in their room they have to move them to another room and keep on moving people to another room and not do anything to fix the original problem until it's absolutely necessary'.

'What a way to run a hotel' said Jeff.

'Sounds a bit to me like they're deliberately running it down for some reason' said Rebecca.

'Did we confirm that the manager on duty that night, Julian Fowler, did have a dentist's appointment the same day the body was discovered?'

'Yes, sir' Ollie confirmed. 'For eleven o'clock that morning at a local dental surgery in Marple. But it also means that the receptionist Anita Patel was alone on duty for an hour before the morning staff started at six'.

'But she said she didn't see or hear anything?' said Jeff.

'That's right, sir' Ollie confirmed.

'Do you think she could be hiding something?'

'Let me say that it wouldn't surprise me but how significant it would be I don't know' said Ollie. 'Like I said before she's nervous about talking to us but I've checked her immigration status and she's not here illegally so she has no reason to be nervous of us. She's doing a business studies degree at Manchester University and working at the hotel to help pay her way'.

'Some of these young people from across the world are so industrious' said Jeff. 'They put some of our own people to shame'.

'They do so' said Ollie.

'Could we be dealing with a grudge against the hotel here?' Rebecca wondered. 'Someone who used to work there for instance? I think it's highly possible given the appalling way the Curzons seem to treat their staff'.

'But a grudge against them that's strong enough to lead to murder?' Jeff questioned. 'Why didn't they murder one of the Curzons in that case?'

'Or maybe there's a connection between Clifton and a former member of staff?' Rebecca pursued. 'They'll have their own reason for murdering Clifton but inconveniencing the hotel by dumping the body there comes as a bonus if they have a grudge against the owners'.

'All of the hotel workers, except for Fowler, are foreign with some from the Indian sub-continent and some from Eastern Europe' said Ollie.

'And all easy to bully' said Rebecca. 'That's why they employ them'.

'Exactly, ma'am' said Ollie.

'Like I said, the rotten bastards' said Rebecca.

'Coming back to the grudge theory though' said Jeff. 'There could be an outside chance so I think it may be worth checking. DC Wright, go through the statements you've gathered from the staff and see if you can make anything from reading between the lines'.

'Will do, sir' said Ollie.

'DS Stockton and I will go and see Alan Travers whose stag party it was' said Jeff. 'And Ollie, see if you can chase up June Hawkins and the forensics report, please. That could give us some tangible clues'.

'Sir, if I may?' said Rebecca. 'When are we, and really I mean when is Ollie here going to get some help with all the computer research donkey work we expect him to do? It isn't fair how much we put on him'.

'Oh I can cope, ma'am' said Ollie.

'I know you can, Ollie, but you shouldn't have to'.

Jeff would have to concede that Rebecca had a point. Ollie had been in need of support for a while but Jeff had a surprise for him and couldn't help grinning rather self-satisfyingly at the news he was about to bestow.

'Funny you should mention that, DS Stockton, because along with the officers being assigned to our MIT we're also getting ourselves our very own computer geek who will be able to do all the boring stuff that I'm sure Ollie will be happy to dump'.

'When do they start, sir?' asked Ollie, his face full of eagerness. He'd love to be able to pass on to someone else some of the computer trawling for information that he found so fucking tedious.

There was a knock at the door and Jeff said. 'Just about now I'd say. Come in!'

Jonathan Freeman came in and greeted everyone.

Except for Ollie who he ignored.

'Sit yourself down, Jonathan' said Jeff.

'Thank you, sir' said Jonathan who'd never had a problem walking into a room full of strangers, especially now he was in such great shape. He'd been to the gym that morning and for a run last night. There were plenty of areas around his flat to exercise and he felt good about his body. He also felt good about starting his new job.

'Punctuality and manners' said Jeff. 'That's a very good start'.

'It's good to see you again, sir' said Jonathan who sat down beside Rebecca.

Rebecca took quite a shine to the fit looking young man. He was hot. He had the kind of cheeky smile you'd forgive anything of. Big hands too, short fair hair and the kind soft blue eyes that really made an impact. A most worthwhile addition to the team in more ways than one and the thought occurred to her that a woman could allow herself a little diversion on her journey to the heart of the one she really wanted. Jeff was still giving off the vibe that he wasn't ready for another relationship yet and Rebecca thought that Jonathan would look very nice inside her whilst she waited. She had no qualms about sleeping with someone just for sex whilst being in love with someone else. This was the twenty-first century after all.

'You'll be reporting to DC Wright here, Jonathan' said Jeff. 'He'll tell you what he needs you to do. And you join us at a frenetic time with a major investigation just started. Think you can handle it?'

'I'll do more than my best, sir' said Jonathan, confidently.

Ollie Wright wondered if Barton or Stockton or any of the others noticed that Jonathan Freeman hadn't shaken his hand in what appeared to be a deliberate act of avoiding him. Ollie tried offering his hand but Freeman took no notice and didn't even make any kind of eye contact with him. It was as if he was pretending that Ollie wasn't there and there were no other black men in the room. He didn't want to jump to conclusions but what was that all about?

FIREFLIES FOUR

Alan Travers shared a house in the Timperley area of Sale in south Manchester with his fiancée and their two kids. Jeff and Rebecca sat with Travers at his kitchen table. His fiancée and the kids who were both under five, were in the living room.

'Lucy just can't get over it' said Alan. 'She's been in a right state. I think we'll postpone the wedding. It just wouldn't feel right to go ahead under the circumstances'.

'How long had you known James Clifton?' asked Rebecca who'd already taken in Alan's physical appearance. He was one of those men who'd begun to lose his hair fairly early and compensated by having it cropped all over so it looked tidy. It made him look a bit like Ross Kemp and he was tall and broad shouldered like him too.

Alan rubbed the stubble on his face. 'We grew up together in Preston' he said softly. He could feel that lump in his throat. 'He was my closest friend. I've got two sisters and he was like the brother I never had. I'm absolutely devastated. We had a great night on the stag do. We were going to fly out to Barcelona or Prague but one or two of them couldn't afford it so we kept local which was fine, like I said, we had a great night. Different girls came and went and all I can remember is that James was there one minute and gone the next'.

'That's what all your friends say too, Alan'.

'Yes, because that's what happened. We all knew James could be a bit of a one with the ladies. God knows he was a good looking bastard and didn't have to try very hard if he was on the pull. But whenever we do all get together we have an agreement that what happens on the night stays on the night if you get my meaning'.

'So you all played away?' Rebecca questioned.

Alan looked round at the door to the room where his fiancée was with the kids. 'No and I don't want you to get that impression. I just meant it's what we'd always agreed but it didn't mean we all took advantage of it'.

'I see' said Rebecca who had no patience with male attitudes to infidelity. 'Thank you for clarifying that'.

'So, what do you do for a living, Alan?' asked Jeff.

'I'm a photographer' Alan explained. 'I run my own business from my office upstairs. I'm not doing too badly considering'.

'What was he like?' asked Jeff.

'Who? James?'

'Yes'.

'Well like I said he was my closest friend which is why he's godfather to our two kids and why I'd asked him to be my best man'.

'Alan, do you know of any reason why anyone would want to kill James?' asked Jeff.

'No! The idea of it ... like I say he wasn't perfect but none of us are'.

'How do you mean he wasn't perfect?' asked Jeff. 'We're just trying to build up an accurate picture of James Clifton to see if it might trigger off something positive in the investigation'.

'No, I do see that, I really do' said Alan who then looked down and stared at his folded hands resting on the table. 'Look, all I can say is that James wasn't entirely reliable when it came to relationships with women. We all thought he'd finally found the right one in Sophie.

We thought she had what it took to satisfy him and stop him from wandering. But it wasn't long before he was back to his old tricks and cheating on her'.

'And this was Sophie Cooper?' Jeff asked as the name bounced round his mind again like a ball hitting every wall in a closed room. Why did that name mean something to him? 'How did Sophie react to that?'

'I don't … I don't want to say anything bad because I like Sophie. She's a great girl in many respects and I think … well that's it really'.

'But?'

'Well she's very needy, very insecure' said Alan. 'There were several times when we all got together and she threw a tantrum followed by tears because she thought he was talking to other people all the time and ignoring her'.

'And was he?' asked Rebecca.

'No, he wasn't' said Alan. 'He was just chatting to everyone like we were all chatting to each other in that kind of social situation. He was just being normal but Sophie wanted him just to talk to her even when he was with all his mates. She's neurotic and she can be very, very moody. She can walk into a happy occasion and suck all the joy out of it straight away. I've seen her do it many times'.

'You just described her as a great girl'.

'Well she is but she has this side to her that really pissed the rest of us off' said Alan. 'And I'm not just talking about the boys. The girls get as pissed off with her as the boys do. She had to have two hundred percent of James' attention all the time and if she thought that she wasn't getting it then there were these flare ups. She threw a pint of beer over him one night in the pub for no other reason than she wanted to go home as soon as they'd got there. James reasoned that they should at least have one drink but she said that he should want to go home just because she wanted to and that he shouldn't argue with her. So she started the tears and he had no patience with that so he ignored her. That's when she threw the beer over him. He had to do exactly what she wanted or there was hell to pay. They both worked shifts and if they had a common day off he would have to do what she'd arranged with no argument or else there'd be a tantrum. If she texted him and he didn't reply straight away then she'd ring him and accuse him of ignoring her. The fact that he might be in the middle of a live TV broadcast made no difference to her. He had to drop everything, including his work, if she snapped her fingers. Unreasonable isn't the word'.

'And yet they were planning to get married?' Rebecca questioned.

'Well' said Alan who rubbed the back of his neck. 'There's a thing. He wanted to break off the engagement and split from Sophie altogether. He just hadn't worked out how or when to break it to her. Because she's so emotionally irrational he didn't know how she'd react. No doubt if he … if James had still been alive he'd have got the third degree from her about what might or might not have happened on the stag night. I wish to God he was here to get that shit from her now'.

'Did they have what you'd call a volatile relationship then?' asked Rebecca.

'Only because she was so neurotic'.

'So you lay the fault entirely at her door?'

'Yes, I do' said Alan who didn't like the look he was getting from Rebecca. It was the look of every woman who believes that whenever a relationship has problems it has to be all the man's fault and anybody who says otherwise is a misogynistic pig. 'And if you knew her you'd think so too.

'But you say he was unfaithful to her?'

'Look he wasn't a serial adulterer' said Alan. 'It happened a couple of times, that's all and it was never more than a one night stand'.

'Oh well that makes it alright then'.

Alan swung on her. 'Look, I've just lost my best friend in horrific circumstances and how dare you sit here in my house and look down on him! Now change your attitude or get out!'

'Alan, let's calm down, shall we?' said Jeff with his hand in the air in a placatory gesture. 'We're not going to get anywhere by losing our rag'.

'Don't address your speech at me' said Alan. 'Give the reprimand to your friend here. James wasn't a bad man despite what she's trying to say'.

'I'm not trying to say anything that would upset you, Alan' said Rebecca who wasn't sure whether she meant that or not. 'And I'm sorry if I caused you any offence'.

'Well I'm not interested in your apology because you shouldn't have said what you did in the first place. He's barely cold and you're pulling him apart. You're despicable. No wonder people are losing confidence in the police'.

'Well that went well' said Jeff as they got back into the car.

'That James Clifton sounds like he was a right bastard' said Rebecca as she fastened her seat-belt. Jeff was driving. 'Men like him think nothing of being unfaithful'.

'You were unprofessional, Rebecca'.

'Oh I was waiting for that'.

'You stamped all over that man's grief, Becky' said Jeff, turning on the ignition. 'You tried to tarnish the memory of his best friend who hasn't been dead five minutes'.

'Yes, well, he said all that'.

'Excuse me?'

'Sorry' said Rebecca. 'I shouldn't have used that tone of voice to you'.

'And the last time I looked infidelity was not a crime punishable by genital mutilation and murder' said Jeff as he indicated and pulled out into the road.

'Perhaps it should be' said Rebecca. 'I can think of many women who'd think so'.

'Well then they'd be wrong, DS Stockton'.

'I thought you had respect for women, sir?'

'And what have I said that's made you doubt that?'

'Well your opinion of James Clifton. I just thought you'd judge him more harshly'.

'Becky, I'm not going to condemn him just because he's a man who didn't keep it in his trousers which is what you seem to want to do' said Jeff. 'And in any case, Sophie Cooper sounds like she's a nightmare to live with'.

'Oh of course it must be the woman's fault'.

'Well you're quite prepared to throw all the blame on James Clifton. Rebecca, in all objectivity it doesn't sound to me like Sophie Cooper behaved much like a woman. More like a spoilt little girl who couldn't stand not to get her own way'.

'He probably drove her to be that way'.

'Rebecca, that statement doesn't make any professional or even personal sense at all. What's got into you?'

'The question supposes that the problem is entirely with me like it is with Sophie Cooper according to Alan Travers'.

Jeff took a deep breath. 'Okay, so what have I done?'

Becky looked at Jeff and felt such an outpouring of feelings that she just couldn't bring herself to have this conversation with him now. This was all such a flaming mess. She just wished he'd react in some way to all the signals she gave off. Any kind of reaction would be good. At least she'd know then that he'd noticed.

'You haven't done anything' she said.

'You've got a funny way of showing it'.

'Look, I'll shake myself out of the bad mood I've been in, Jeff' said Rebecca. 'I had a row with my sister yesterday and then another one with my mother this morning because she took my sister's side like she always does. It just pissed me off but I'll get over it'.

'You were okay until Alan Travers started being critical of Sophie Cooper'.

'Well maybe I'd just like to hear her side of things' said Rebecca. 'I've been on the receiving end of men who treat women badly and then wonder why they get upset'.

'Men feel pain too, Becky'.

'Yes, I know Jeff but men are far more likely to be unfaithful than women'.

'I think that depends on the man and the woman'.

'Well men are hopeless about admitting to what they've done. That's why I went to Sophie Cooper's defence because she was being got at by Alan Travers'.

'Because he knows her and you don't' said Jeff.

'Can't you give me a day off from being perfect?'

Jeff laughed. 'Well, alright. But don't take a week's leave on it'.

An awkward silence fell on them that lasted for the rest of the journey back to the station leaving Jeff totally unconvinced that Becky had told him anything like the whole truth.

'Look' said Jeff before Rebecca got out of the car. 'Are we good, Becky?'

'Yeah, yeah we're good, Jeff'.

'I hope so, Becky. I really do. You're a good friend and a valued friend. I'd hate to lose that'.

Sharon Bellfield was trying to figure out where the hell she was. She could hear her phone ringing somewhere. Why had she changed the ring tone to that irritatingly banal Ellie Goulding piece of crap going burn, burn, fucking burn all the time? She reached out from underneath the darkness and realised she was in a bed. It wasn't her bed. So whose was it? She had to go into a semi fight with the duvet to get the thing from being wrapped round her like a fucking python. She opened a bleary eye and reached out for where she could see her phone vibrating on the bedside table but her hand fell short. A bedside table? That was a bit domestic for the men she liked to go with. Rough and ready types who showed a girl a good time was what she was partial to and they tended to have a bed in the bedroom and not much else.

She could barely remember being in that last bar and looking at her watch seeing it was after half past two. That last vodka and coke had been a mistake. She could feel something beside her. Something was breathing. This was no good. Thirty-three years old and waking up in someone's bed with a hangover from hell and having no idea where she was. It had got to stop.

'Are you going to get that fucking phone?'

The voice was aggressive but female. Oh no, thought Sharon. When was she going to learn that if she couldn't find a man to get off with she shouldn't fall for the charms of the nearest lesbian. She'd always had a bit of a lesbian fan club. It came from her being slightly on the butch side but she wasn't a lesbian or even just a little bit bisexual. She liked men. She just couldn't find one with a bed with a table beside it.

'Sorry' croaked Sharon. She edged further towards the end of the bed and this time managed to grab the phone to her ear.

'Sharon?'

'Get your arse down here pronto'.

'Oh good morning to you, Ken'.

'You were supposed to be here ninety minutes ago. I can't keep covering for you, Sharon. I don't care where you are or what state you're in. Get yourself here. I've got a job for you'.

Sharon pressed the end call button and rubbed her face. Ken was a good sort. Shame he was old enough to be her Dad and had been happily married for thirty years. He was just the kind of man she needed because he took no crap from her and told her in no uncertain terms when she was out of order. This was another morning in a long line of mornings when she felt like shit. She'd get through it. She wondered what kind of job he had for her. Bless him. Even though she gave him so much bother he did tend to give her some juicy stuff to do.

'I think you should go now, please' said the woman next to her as she got out of bed and walked round to the door in the corner. Sharon could see she was quite a fit looking bird with shoulder length red hair and big well defined tits that were much better than her own.

'I'm sorry if I passed out'.

'I don't mind you passing out. What I mind is you using me for sex tourism. You were useless in bed. I might've known you weren't gay'.

'Could you tell me where I am?'

'You're in the northern quarter a couple of blocks from Piccadilly gardens' said the woman before disappearing into the bathroom and slamming the door shut behind her.

'I suppose a coffee is out of the question?' Sharon shouted. Her request was greeted with silence. 'I'll take that as a no then'.

FIREFLIES FIVE

Jeff got himself showered and dressed before seeing to Toby and preparing breakfast whilst his son was watching the cartoon channel on their TV set in the kitchen diner. They both had toast with cheese spread on and whilst Toby went for coco pops, Jeff made himself the kind of instant porridge that you just add boiling water to. Toby had a cup of Chinese tea which he'd really taken to after his grandparents had introduced him to it and Jeff had a mug of earl grey with a slice of lemon. As they sat around the breakfast table talking and consuming Jeff was acutely aware, as he always is, of who was missing. It was as if there was an empty space in every room of the house since Lillie Mae died.

'Toby, would you mind if someone came to live here who could look after you when I'm at work?'

Toby looked up at his father quizzically. 'Have you got a girlfriend, Daddy?'

Jeff smiled. 'No, mate, I haven't got a girlfriend but when I do I promise you'll be the first to know'.

'So what's up, Daddy?'

'Well I think we need someone here all the time'.

'You mean we'd get a servant like in Downton Abbey? They couldn't live downstairs though because there isn't enough room in that little cupboard and they wouldn't be able to breathe'.

Jeff ruffled his son's jet black hair. 'No, they wouldn't be like a servant, mate. They'd be more like a friend who was here to take care of both of us'.

'But we've got Uncle Lewis and Uncle Seamus to do that. Don't they want to do it anymore?'

'Of course they do, of course they do' Jeff reassured. 'We'd still see Uncle Lewis and Seamus as much as we do now. It would just make life easier when I get called out to go to work at short notice. I mean, do you remember that time I had to run you round to Pam's in your pyjamas and dressing gown?'

'Yeah but I didn't mind' said Toby who was shaking his legs up and down under the table. 'I got to have breakfast with Stephen and Jennifer and Pam made pancakes with strawberries. She says I'm cute as Christmas'.

Jeff laughed. 'And she's right you are, mate'.

'So what's the problem?'

'Well Pam might not always be there when we need her' said Jeff. 'But if someone lived here then neither of us would ever have to worry'.

Toby sat and thought for a moment. 'Okay'.

'Really?'

'Yeah' said Toby. 'Why not? It might be fun'.

'Okay, well your Uncle Lewis and Uncle Seamus have got a mate called Brendan who wants to make a living out of caring for people like me and you'.

'You mean people without a Mummy?'

Jeff brought his hand up to his mouth and gulped. 'That's it, mate'.

'Well then okay get him to come round' said Toby. 'If he can play xbox and cook as good as Uncle Lewis can then he'll be sound. On one condition though?'

'What's that, mate?'

Toby slid off his chair and got on his Daddy's knee. Jeff put his arms round him. 'After Mummy died you said we'd always be the A team?'

'Yeah and we always will?'

'So if someone else comes to live with us then we'll still be that A team, Daddy?'

'Of course we will' said Jeff. 'Nobody else gets to be part of our A team'.

'Daddy?'

'Yes, mate?'

'Are you missing Mummy?'

Jeff had to take another deep breath before answering. 'Yes, mate. I am missing Mummy'.

'Well you've still got me'.

Jeff kissed the top of Toby's head. 'I know mate and that makes me the luckiest Daddy in the whole world'.

Jeff dropped Toby off at school and then drove into work. When he got to the station he sat in his car for a few minutes to try and compose himself. Grief was such a long and drawn out process and recently he thought he'd been doing okay. But it wasn't as simple as that.

Just when he thought he might be starting to come to terms with it he'd woken up that morning and been struck by an emotion that was as crushing as the day he'd been told that Lillie Mae had died.

But he also had a case to think about and he simply didn't believe that the body of a grown man could be dumped at the back of a large hotel without anybody noticing. Someone had carefully planned the murder of James Clifton. He was certain of that much. But was James Clifton the actual target or did he just happen to fit the profile of whatever the killer was looking for? Was he simply in the wrong place at the wrong time? It's rarely as simple as that in Jeff's experience but they needed to delve more deeply into Clifton's background to see if he'd done anything that might go some way towards explaining the horror of his fate. Then there was the familiarity he felt about the name of Sophie Cooper. He still hadn't worked out why that meant something to him and it was still driving him mad.

'Sir?' said Ollie as Jeff walked through the squad room in the direction of his office. 'We have the report from June Hawkins'.

Jeff carried on walking and then realised that Ollie had just spoken to him. 'Yeah? Sorry Ollie, I'm miles away'.

'Sir, there was enough rohipnol in James Clifton's blood to have completely knocked him out for hours. It's likely that he wouldn't have known anything'.

'Lucky him in that case' said Jeff. 'Anything else?'

'Oh yes' said Ollie' I've got something to show you'.

'Good news or bad news?'

'Oh I think you'll like it, sir' said Ollie who was worried about the way the boss looked. 'Are you okay, sir?'

Jeff smiled. 'Yeah, I'm fine, Ollie, I'm fine' he said as he stood behind his desk. 'Go on?'

Ollie then slid a DVD into the computer on Jeff's desk. 'Sir, this is the last image of James Clifton we could find on any of the CCTV sources for that area of the city centre. It clearly shows him walking in the direction of Lower Mosley Street and away from the Paradise club where we'd seen him going in an hour earlier with the rest of his party'.

'Yes' said Jeff as he eyed the images on the screen and suddenly felt excited. 'And he's not alone'.

'Exactly, sir' said Ollie. 'And that could be the moment when James Clifton first meets his killer'.

Ollie Wright had no time for people who play the race card to mask their incompetence. He'd seen it happen. He had a cousin who was the laziest bitch in the world but when her boss threatened her with disciplinary action if she didn't pull her socks up and stop letting everyone else in the office where she worked carry her, she was proud of the fact that she'd replied with 'I'm black and I'm a woman. That means I've two ace cards against a white middle-aged man like you. So who do you think an industrial tribunal would believe if you dared to try and sack me?' Ollie had been disgusted with her behavior. She made it even more difficult for black people who really were the victims of racism to plead their case.

He knew that racism existed in the police force but he also tried not to find it hiding under every bush. That's why he was struggling with Jonathan Freeman. The squad's new computer geek who hadn't shaken hands with him or even looked him in the eye on the day he joined the team, didn't look anything like a geek at all but had been making remarks that had made Ollie stop and wonder if he was being deliberately wound up. Jonathan only made the remarks within Ollie's hearing and it was making Ollie feel uncomfortable about being with him.

'Tell me' said Jonathan. 'How do you feel when you have to investigate your own people?' He was inputting to the computer some of the findings from the door-to-door enquiries that uniform had started around the Mayfair hotel. He was sitting opposite Ollie with whom he was sharing a desk.

Ollie looked away from his own computer screen and paused irritably. He never knew where Freeman's remarks were going to end up. 'Excuse me?'

'Well with so many crimes committed by your people' Jonathan went on. 'Statistically speaking'.

'What do you expect me to say to that?'

'No need to be so sensitive'.

'Who said I was being sensitive?'

'It's written all over your face, mate'.

Ollie closed his eyes for a moment. How did we go from zero to a hundred in such little time? 'Just tell me why you asked me that?'

'Well I just meant that investigating your people might be personally compromising for you'.

'My people?'

'Yeah'.

'You mean black people?'

'Hey, listen mate, don't try and lay the big discrimination ticket on me because I was only taking a friendly interest between colleagues and if you read it as something else then I question your impartiality and professional judgment'.

'I beg your pardon?'

'Well if you don't realise you're doing it, mate, then perhaps it does need to be pointed out to you'.

'Doing what for God's sake?'

'Well you're clearly sensitive about the whole race issue'.

'Actually I'm not sensitive about it at all'.

'Well you would say that, mate, wouldn't you, but the evidence of what you say and how you react suggests to me something quite different'.

'And you think you have a right to say such crap to me because?'

'Oh am I not allowed to voice my opinion? Oh well I'm sorry but I thought this was Great Britain but where you come from the situation is probably different'.

'I come from Rochdale' said Ollie through gritted teeth.

Jonathan waved his hand in the air dismissively. 'Yeah, yeah, whatever'.

Ollie didn't know how best to react to Freeman's goading. Bastards like Freeman were very clever and they tended to make sure that their victim ended up looking like an immature and overly sensitive soul at best or the villain of the piece at worst. He sat there seething. Freeman had this evil look on his face, like he was about to join a firing squad and had to focus on 'the kill'. Ollie stood up and went to get some air. He really didn't need this.

When Tina got to work she was immediately confronted by the manager Paula Jones.

'Do you really think I'm going to let you work here today, Tina?' demanded Paula.

Tina looked at her guardedly. She knew exactly what Paula meant. She felt sick. 'What do you mean?'

'Don't play the bloody innocent with me! It was you, wasn't it? It was you in the CCTV footage they showed on the evening news walking away with that man who ended up dead?'

'I don't know what you're talking about'.

'Don't talk crap! I want you to go home until this matter is settled and then we'll review your future employment with this company'.

'So much for supportive management' said Tina. 'And do you think I could've killed someone?'

Paula shrugged her shoulders. 'I don't know what you're capable of. I've only known you five minutes'.

'You bitch'.

'Er, excuse me, lady, you don't get to call the shots when you could've brought this store into your obviously sordid private life'.

'How fucking dare you speak to me like that!'

'I dare because my own son is going out on his stag night this coming weekend' said Paula. 'It says in the papers that the killer might be targeting stag parties for their own twisted reasons and I have a duty to my son to protect him when it was clearly you who was walking away with Saturday's victim. You can deny your involvement all you like but I'm only going to speak to you if there are other people present like there is now'.

Tina looked round and spotted several of her colleagues looking on with barely disguised embarrassment. 'What kind of person do you think I am for God's sake?'

'One who can't work here whilst you've got this hanging over your head' said Paula, firmly.

'That's not fair' said Tina who then started to cry. She'd seen the footage on the news. It had kept her awake all night. 'I didn't kill him. I couldn't kill anyone'.

Just at that moment the door to the staff room opened and two figures walked in who made Tina gasp with panic when they introduced themselves.

'I'm Detective superintendent Jeff Barton and this is my colleague Detective sergeant Rebecca Stockton' said Jeff as both he and Rebecca held up their warrant cards.

'And I'm Paula Jones, the store manager' Paula announced with her usual affected smile. 'I think you must be here to speak to my staff member Tina Webb here'.

Tina glared at Paula before turning her eyes to the detectives and asking meakly. 'What do you want with me?'

'Tina, we received a phone call this morning identifying you as the girl in the CCTV footage walking arm in arm with James Clifton out of the Paradise club on the night he was murdered. We need to ask you some questions'.

'You can have my office for as long as you like, detectives' said Paula.

'Thank you but I'm afraid that due to the seriousness of the matter we think it's best if Miss Webb accompanies us to the station'.

'Are you arresting me?' asked Tina.

'We're asking you to assist us with our enquiries, Tina' said Jeff. 'And if you didn't kill James Clifton then you've got nothing to worry about'.

FIREFLIES SIX

Jeff managed to put aside his slide back into conscious grieving in order to concentrate on what was emerging in the case. He went into the interview room with Rebecca where Tina Webb was sitting waiting for them. She looked up anxiously when they sat down opposite her with the table in between and switched on the tape recorder. Tina was frightened. She'd never seen the inside of a police station before.

'Tina, we're interviewing you under caution in connection with the murder of James Clifton' said Jeff. 'Do you understand what that means?'

'I didn't kill him'.

'You've already waived your right to legal representation' said Jeff. 'Do you wish to confirm that decision?'

'I didn't kill him so why would I need a lawyer?'

'Okay' said Jeff who then proceeded to read Tina her rights.

'This is mad' said Tina. 'Who told you it was me on the CCTV?'

'Oh I'm afraid we can't tell you that, Tina' said Jeff.

Tina had a bloody good idea who it would've been. It must've been Paula Jones, the fucking bitch. 'Am I being charged with something?'

'Not at this point, no' said Jeff. 'Did you go out with friends on Saturday night or were you on your own?'

'There were three of us, me, my friend Andrea Kay from work and my friend Donna Price'.

'We'll need their contact details'.

'Well you can find Andrea at the supermarket where I work on Regent Road. Donna works in an insurance office in town. She's not a snob though like some of them office girls can be'.

'Did you all go your separate ways on Saturday night?'

'Well we were together until more or less the same time' said Tina. 'I'm the only one who pulled though. Andrea doesn't really do that sort of thing. She's more of a looker than a player. Donna is normally up for it but she just wasn't in the mood that night. They shared a taxi home because they don't live too far away from each other and they both texted me to say they'd got home okay'.

'How long were you talking to James Clifton before you left the club with him?'

'About an hour or so' said Tina. 'I mean I can't be precise because it was well into the night and we'd all had a few'.

'Which one of you suggested you go off together?'

'He did' said Tina. 'Andrea and Donna were talking to a couple of the others in the stag party but like I said they didn't go back with anyone'.

'Tina, you know about the CCTV footage we have of you leaving the Paradise club with James Clifton on Saturday night' said Jeff.

'I do, yes' Tina replied in a soft voice.

'Around four hours later his mutilated body was found behind a rubbish bin at the back of the Mayfair hotel in Stockport'.

'I've never even been to that hotel' Tina declared. 'I've never been anywhere near it and that's the truth'.

'What happened after the two of you left the club, Tina?' Rebecca asked.

'He came back to mine' Tina admitted in a soft voice. 'But look, I swear I didn't kill him. You've got to believe me'.

'So what did happen between you?' asked Jeff. 'The sooner you tell us that the sooner we can get this over with'.

Tina's moment of inner bravado from moments ago had gone. Inside she was trembling and was beginning to regret her earlier decision not to have a lawyer present. 'I poured us each a glass of wine. I thought he was going to stay a while but he ended up only staying half an hour or so'.

'Why was that?'

Tina gulped down some water before recalling the uncomfortable situation that developed that night with James Clifton. 'He wanted me to do something sexually that I wasn't prepared to do. He kept on insisting and I kept on refusing and eventually he just kind of lost it. I don't know how else to put it really'.

When James Clifton got through Tina's front door they were all over each other. It was frenzied, drunken, like many of Tina's sexual encounters and it wasn't long before they were both naked and entwined on Tina's sofa.

'I'll bet you're a filthy little bitch' said James.

'I have my moments'.

Tina knew what she was doing as she went down on James and stuck her finger up his ass but then he said he wanted her to piss on him.

'I don't do that' said Tina.

'What do you mean you don't do that?'

'I can show you a good time but not like that'.

'I want you to piss on me, Tina'.

'Well I'm sorry but I don't do that'.

'Don't be such a fucking baby. You walk into the club tonight dressed like everything is on offer and now you turn into a prude?'.

'I am not a prude. I just don't do that'.

'Fucking prick tease'.

'Hey, now just a minute, James. What's got into you?'

James got off the sofa and started looking for his clothes. 'I'll tell you what's got into me. Its selfish little bitches like you who won't give men like me what we want'.

Something about the tone in James's voice and the manner with which he was now grabbing his clothes off the floor was really unnerving Tina. How had it all gone so wrong? It was like there was a different person in the flat from only a few minutes ago.

'Where are you going, James?'

'Away from all the schizophrenic little bitches like you'.

'James, I don't understand. I thought you wanted me'.

'I pick up tarts like you because I want something different. I can get all the usual kind of shit at home. I want something different from the likes of you'.

'The likes of me?'

'Oh don't be offended when you were making it pretty clear tonight that your legs were ready and willing to be opened'.

'Well I'm sorry if you're disappointed'.

'So am I for having wasted my bloody time. Where's my fucking shirt?'

'It's in the hall' said Tina who now wanted James out of there as quickly as possible.

'Oh don't fucking look at me like that' said James.

'Like what?'

'Like I'm the big, bad boy'.

'Well it isn't me who's ruined what could've been a good time'.

'Oh listen to yourself' said James, scathingly. 'You're acting like a teenage girl'.

'I don't know what's got into you'.

'Oh yeah? Well let me clarify my position'.

James slapped Tina across the face so hard it knocked her off balance and she fell to the ground sideways.

'Get out!' Tina demanded.

'Oh don't worry I'm going' said James. 'Where can I find a cab?'

'There'll be plenty around this time. Just go down to the main road'.

Tina finished her explanation of that fateful night to Jeff and Rebecca who were both making notes to question James Clifton's girlfriend to see if there was any history of domestic violence in her relationship with Clifton. Tina then asked if she could go.

'Not yet, I'm afraid, no' said Rebecca.

'But that was the last I saw of him, I swear to you'.

'What do you think happened after that?'

'I don't know'

'How were you feeling?'

'Initially frightened that he'd come back and have a real go at me and then as time passed I started to calm down a bit'.

'And how do you feel now?'

'Well now he's dead and the circumstances … well I don't know but I can't stop thinking about him. If he hadn't been so intent on getting what he wanted then he would've stayed for a while and then just gone home I expect. And he'd still have been alive. I just can't believe things turned out the way they did, detective. I've had loads of men and I don't deny it. That night wasn't unlike any other when all I wanted was some fun'.

'And it ends like this?'

'Yes' said Tina who then started to cry.

'With a man dead who you'd been personally intimate with'.

'Yes' said Tina who was drying her eyes with a tissue. 'It sends a shiver down my spine I can tell you'.

'Why?' Jeff wanted to know. 'Because you're afraid you might get caught?'

'Caught for what? I haven't done anything'.

'So you say' Rebecca sneered.

'Yes I say because it's true! I didn't kill him!'

'But some might say you had reason to?' said Rebecca. 'He'd been violent towards you because you'd refused to perform a specific sexual act'.

Tina felt like she was cracking up. She couldn't believe they were trying to get her to confess to the murder of this man. 'I don't know what else to say' she whimpered. 'I didn't kill him. I swear to God it happened just like I said'.

'Did anybody see James Clifton leaving your flat?' asked Rebecca.

'I don't know' said Tina, still trying to wipe her cheeks dry. 'Will you need to ask everyone in the block and in the street?'

'Yes, that'll be unavoidable I'm afraid'.

'Oh my God, they'll all think I did it'.

'And we'll need to get a warrant to search your flat, Tina' said Rebecca.

'Tina' said Jeff, leaning forward with his hands clasped on the table between them. 'You've got to help us here but you've also got to help yourself'.

'But I haven't done anything!'

'Even so, I'd strongly advise you to seek legal advice'.

Tina was crying her heart out. 'He left my flat and I don't know what happened to him after that. I really can't tell you anymore'.

Jonathan Freeman watched from a distance as DC Ollie Wright laughed and shared a joke with two of the other officers on the squad. Because Jonathan was a civilian member of the squad he was excluded from a lot of the 'in' jokes. He presumed they thought he wouldn't understand. How wrong they were.

He noticed that Ollie Wright had left his wallet on his desk. Freeman looked around and when he was sure that the coast was clear he reached for it. He shoved it into his pocket and then went to the gents. Inside one of the cubicles he opened it up. There were the usual bank and credit cards, boring stuff that wouldn't be of any use, a gym membership card. Why did so many black men use the bloody gym for God's sake? A couple of return rail tickets to be used up and then, tucked away in a small buttoned down pocket was a picture that was worth its weight in gold for Jonathan. He couldn't help smiling. He'd got him. But he was going to save it for another day. He had other plans for this particular incident.

He went back out to the squad room where Ollie was frantically looking for his wallet.

'Is this what you're looking for?' he asked as he held the wallet in the air between them.

'Where did you find that?' Ollie asked.

'In the corridor, mate' said Jonathan. 'It must've slipped out your pocket'.

Ollie stared at him. 'Is that right?'

'Hey, don't look at me like that, mate' said Freeman in a voice raised up so that the rest of the office would hear. 'I mean are you accusing me of stealing it or something?'

'I'm not saying anything of the sort' said Ollie, suddenly aware that the room had gone quiet. They must all be listening and Freeman had timed it perfectly. 'Don't put words in my mouth'.

'Do you know what? I'm getting to really resent your attitude towards me'.

Ollie could've laughed. 'My attitude towards you?'

'And there you go again turning it on me' said Freeman. 'Look, don't communicate with me unless it's about the work, mate, okay? Because you clearly have an issue with me personally and I'm just not going to allow you to abuse me in that way'. He paused and when he was sure the rest of the office had turned back to what they'd been doing he leaned forward towards a startled Ollie and whispered. 'So next time you're at your black policeman's association dinner remember that racism goes both ways and you're not going to bully me into a submissive belief in a so-called multi-cultural society so don't even try'.

Ollie was completely lost for words and sat down heavily in his chair.

'Okay, Tina' said Jeff Barton after he and Rebecca had come back into the interview room armed with some new information that the search team had discovered at Tina Webb's flat. Tina was now sitting with a solicitor beside her but it hadn't taken away the look of sheer terror on her face. Jeff reminded her that she was still under caution.

'You've kept me here for hours' said Tina. 'You can't keep me here all this time it's not fair'.

'Fair on who, Tina?' Rebecca asked. 'You or James Clifton?'

Tina was exasperated with this line of questioning. 'I kept telling you before that I don't know what happened to James Clifton. Why won't you believe me?'

'We've searched your flat, Tina' Jeff continued. 'I'm afraid it's now a lot more serious than before'.

'Why?' asked Tina in a panicked voice. 'You won't have found anything there that makes me look like a murderer'.

'For the benefit of the tape I'm holding two clear plastic bags, one with a foil wrapped strip of tablets and the other with a blood stained kitchen knife in it' said Jeff. 'Are these items yours, Tina?'

'No, I've … I've got no idea'.

'Well that's strange because they were found in your flat' said Rebecca.

'They can't have been!'

'We're not in the habit of lying, Tina' said Rebecca. 'We leave all that to the criminals'.

'The drug is Rohipnol' said Jeff. 'It's more commonly known as the date rape drug. And the blood on the rather large knife which looks more like a meat cleaver to me has been confirmed by forensics as being that of James Clifton'.

Tina burst into tears. 'This isn't happening. I don't know anything about these things'.

'But they were found in your flat, Tina' Rebecca repeated.

'Yes, I know, I heard you the first time but I don't know anything about them!'

'Why did you kill him in such a violent way, Tina?' asked Rebecca.

'I don't know what you're talking about'.

'Was it because he'd hit you?' Rebecca went on. 'Anybody would've reacted badly to that, Tina. Nobody would blame you if you'd decided to hit back'.

'But I didn't'.

'Why did you invite him back to your place, Tina?'

'Because I liked the look of him'.

'And?'

'Because I wanted to have sex with him'.

'And the object of your desire slapped you for your troubles'.

'I told him to get out, that's all'.

'You were affronted. He'd crushed your pride. You were ready to give him the night of his life and all he wanted you to do was piss on him'.

'The filthy bastard'.

'Yes, Tina, the filthy, perverted bastard'.

'I wanted him out of there'.

'You wanted to kill him'.

'I did not!'

'Come on, Tina. It's understandable'.

'Look' said the solicitor, Ryan Kershaw. He hadn't been qualified for long but he'd attended several of these police interviews and had already worked with Detective Superintendent Jeff Barton and Detective sergeant Rebecca Stockton. He had some respect for them both but he didn't think that Tina Webb was guilty of anything other than liking men even though the evidence was beginning to say otherwise. 'You're trying to lead my client into a confession for something she hasn't done and has told you repeatedly that she hasn't. Now back off, detectives or I'll advise my client not to answer anymore of your questions'.

'Come on, Tina' said Rebecca. 'You were seen walking off with James Clifton, you admit taking him back to your flat where he physically abused you, then we find Rohipnol in your flat together with a knife with Clifton's blood all over it'.

'And I don't know how any of that stuff got there' pleaded Tina. She was sobbing so much it was making her shake. 'I wouldn't even know what Rohipnol looked like'.

'Do you really expect us to believe that, Tina?'

'Believe what you like'.

'You're starting to sound boring now, Tina'.

'That's because you're just not listening!'

'What offends you about stag nights, Tina?'

'Nothing offends me about them'.

'You knew that James Clifton was on a stag night'.

'What's that got to do with anything?' Tina blurted out between sobs.

'Did you add the Rohipnol to the glass of wine you poured him? We know it was in his system'.

'No!'

'But if you don't know anything about the Rohipnol or the blood stained knife then how do you explain how they got into your flat?'

Tina almost screamed her answer. 'I don't know! Look, talk to my family, talk to my friends. They'll all tell you I couldn't possibly be involved in anything like this'

'Can we take a five minute break, detective?' asked Ryan. 'You can see how distressed my client is getting'.

'Yes, well murder does tend to get rather distressing for the victim especially when he gets his genitals hacked off in the process of being murdered' said Rebecca.

'And we can do without remarks like that, detective' said Ryan.

'We'll take a break now, Tina' said Jeff. 'We need to make some further enquiries'.

'Please let me go'

'We'll make those enquiries and then we'll come back to you, Tina' said Jeff. 'But be prepared to stay here tonight'.

FIREFLIES SEVEN

Jeff pinned pictures of Tina Webb and her two friends Andrea Kay and Donna Price onto the clear plastic mission board in the middle of the squad room.

'Statements have been taken from both of Tina Webb's fellow travelers from the night in question' said Jeff. 'Ollie? What did they tell us?'

'Well both Andrea Kay and Donna Price confirm that they shared a taxi that went first to Andrea's home in Crumpsall and then to Donna Price's home in Middleton, sir' said Ollie. 'The taxi firm has confirmed the journey and the phone companies have confirmed the text messages that both girls sent to Tina to say they were both safely home'.

'Do you think she did it, sir?' asked Rebecca.

'Well the evidence suggests that she at least had something to do with it but looking beyond that evidence I'm yet to be convinced that she could single-handedly seduce someone into her flat and end up cutting their balls off. I mean, can you?'

'I admit there's a lot of holes in the probabilities and that means the whole thing doesn't make much sense' said Rebecca. 'But if she was working with someone else then who and why? Either she's too scared to say or we've got it all wrong and she's more dangerous than she looks'.

'Well we've still got some time left' said Jeff. 'Ollie? Look again at the CCTV from inside the Paradise club. Try and compare the behaviour of Tina Webb and that of her two friends'.

'Sir'.

'DS Stockton? Let's go and see Andrea Kay and Donna Price'.

Jeff drove the short distance from the station to the supermarket up on Regent Road in Salford to interview Andrea Kay and Rebecca decided to use the time to do some interviewing of her own.

'So how did Toby enjoy his weekend with his grandparents?'

'He had a great time, thanks' said Jeff. 'He's driving me and our Lewis mad with his social life. He's always got to be here, there and everywhere. He's going to spend this weekend too with Lillie Mae's parents. They've got family over from Hong Kong and they want to show him off'.

'You won't know what to do with yourself'.

'You're right' said Jeff, quietly. 'Although it depends on how this case builds. I'll probably sleep my way through much of it to be honest because I'm knackered'.

'That's no life for someone in their mid thirties, Jeff'.

'Maybe not' said Jeff. 'But it's the life I'm in and I've got to make the best of it for Toby's sake. He's got to grow up as happy as he can be without his Mum around'.

'You wouldn't be selfish if you thought about what you needed once in a while'.

'Well this is just my way of dealing with things at the moment, Becky. I didn't expect to lose my wife when we'd only been married four years and had a beautiful baby boy. We'd have probably had more children and it isn't fair but then life isn't and we come across that all the time in our job'.

'I just don't want you to deny yourself the chance to be happy if that chance came along'.

'Don't worry about me, Becky' said Jeff. 'But I do have to be careful about who I let into my life in future. I come as a package with the best little boy in the world. Any woman is going to have to accept that'.

'But Jeff, a woman who's worthwhile will fall in love with you the man first, not you the father. Only then will she be able to give her best to the both of you'.

Jeff paused for a moment. Becky made a lot of sense with what she was saying but he couldn't even contemplate being with another woman yet. He had been thinking that his carnal needs were beginning to open the door on his reluctance to get involved with someone again. But in fact all it had done was tell him that he was missing sex and he wasn't the sort of man who could treat a woman like a prostitute. It wasn't only women who thought that the best sex came out of genuine and mutual feelings between two people.

'Anyway, what about you? You haven't been seeing anybody for a while. Anybody on the horizon?'

'Jonathan Freeman asked me out the other day'.

'I thought you two were getting along rather well' said Jeff who'd also noted a spot of tension between Freeman and Ollie Wright. He didn't know what it was about but he wasn't going to mention it to Rebecca if she had romantic inclinations towards Freeman. 'You should go for it'.

'I should?'

'Well he's fit, good-looking, and even he laughs at my jokes. Yeah, go for it. Life is short. Trust me, I know'.

'This is not a formal interview, Andrea' said Rebecca as the three of them sat in the manager Paula Jones' office. 'We're just checking up on some enquiries with regard to your friend Tina Webb?' We understand that she's one of your best friends?

'Yes she is' Andrea confirmed, proudly. 'But I've already made a statement'.

'And we're just following that up'.

Andrea was incredulous. 'Oh please don't tell me you really think Tina murdered James Clifton?'

'Well why do you think that assumption would be wrong?' asked Jeff.

'Because she couldn't kill anybody' Andrea insisted. 'It's barmy'.

'What is she like?' asked Rebecca.

'Tina? Well she's kind, she's loyal and she's funny. I confide everything about my life in Tina because I trust her'.

'And is she like that with all of her friends?'

'Well I can't imagine why she wouldn't be because she's just like that'.

'Would anyone seek to repay that loyalty by lying for her?'

'Hey now just a minute' said Andrea. 'Don't you try and put words in my mouth to give you the answer you want'.

'I was merely asking you a direct and straightforward question, Andrea'.

'Rubbish. You were trying to get me to say something negative about my friend'.

'She says you don't go out on the pull in the same way that she does'

'Oh so now you're painting her as a slut, are you?'

'No, Andrea' said Rebecca slowly. 'I just want an answer to my question, please'.

'Well alright I wish I could be more of a free spirit like she is but I'm not' Andrea stated.

'Can you tell us how the evening panned out on Saturday?'

Andrea gave them a virtually identical version of what Tina had told them and about what they'd already given in their initial statements.

'Do you live by yourself?'

'No' said Andrea. 'I fell out with my father and step-mother a long time ago and went to live with my Gran and I still live there. She can vouch that I got home at half two just like I said in my statement because she always waits up for me, bless her. It is a bit of a passion killer when it comes to wanting to go home with a man but I don't get the offers like Tina does, or even Donna, so it's rarely a problem really'.

'It sounds like you and Tina are absolute opposites' said Rebecca.

'Oh we are but I think that makes for a good friendship' said Andrea. 'Look, Tina is a tart with a heart. She just couldn't do something as horrible as that. She likes men. Somebody who does something like that clearly doesn't'.

'Have you ever seen any sign of anything untoward happening in her life?' Rebecca pursued.

'Untoward? How do you mean?'

'Well has she ever tried to be secretive about anything?'

'Not that I've ever noticed' said Andrea. 'Quite the reverse. She's an open book. She never leaves any details out when she's telling you about her exploits with men'.

'So she has an active life where men are concerned?'

'Oh yes' said Andrea. 'Like I told you, she likes men'.

'But there's nobody special in her life?'

'No' said Andrea. 'I think she'd like there to be but she hasn't met the right one yet and she's having a bloody good time whilst she waits. Nothing wrong with that'.

'No, absolutely' said Rebecca. 'Did she have any bad experiences with men? Experiences that would've left her bitter or even damaged in some way?'

'Not that I know of, no'.

'So what do you think would motivate her to kill someone?'

'Nothing' said Andrea, adamantly. 'She is not a killer and I'll go on repeating that until it gets through to you'.

'You were the acting manager here, weren't you, Andrea?' said Jeff after skimming his eyes over a document he'd read a few minutes before Andrea Kay came in to be interviewed.

'Yes, I was'.

'And during that time you put Tina in charge of the meat counter'.

'Yes?'

'Why did you do that?'

'Because I needed someone to fill that post and I admit that I promoted my mate because I felt she deserved a chance that she hadn't previously been given to run her own section'.

'I see' said Jeff. 'During that time certain pieces of equipment went missing, didn't they? I'm talking about several small meat cutting knives and at least two large meat chopping blades that look more to me like cleavers'.

'So what are you saying?'

'I'm asking if you ever got to the bottom of what happened to that stock?'

'No we didn't'.

'So what do you think happened to them?'

'I've no idea'.

'Well you see I'm just wondering if you covered up for Tina then and are still covering up for her now?'

When Jeff and Rebecca got back to the office DC Ollie Wright told them that a bag of clothes had been found in some undergrowth to the side of the Mayfair hotel car park. They match what James Clifton is seen wearing in the CCTV footage and they're covered in Tina Webb's fingerprints and DNA.

'What did Andrea Kay say about the knives, sir?' asked Ollie.

'Well she was rather embarrassed about it in the end' said Jeff. 'But she did cover up their disappearance because Tina was her friend. She said that Tina was setting up a new flat at the time and she wanted to help her because she didn't have much cash to buy things for it'.

'I don't have meat cleavers in my flat' said Ollie. 'But the one with James Clifton's blood all over it and the smaller knives were all found in Tina Webb's flat, tucked away at the back of a cupboard in her bedroom. Could they have been planted by the real killer?'

'Well she says that the only other people to have a key to her flat are her parents' said Rebecca. 'Unless they've got something to do with this which I doubt'.

'I think you've got a point though, Ollie'.

'Unless we're being fooled by this vulnerable tart with a heart act' said Rebecca. 'She was the last one seen with James Clifton, there's absolutely no sighting of him leaving her flat on his own, no taxi companies have said that they picked him up and a meat cleaver with Clifton's blood on it was in her flat and she has no explanation for any of it. Now we've found a bag of clothes which look like they belonged to James Clifton and have got her DNA all over them. We've charged people on a lot less, sir'.

'Added to all that though, Rebecca, there's no sign of any struggle in Tina Webb's flat and no sign of Clifton's blood there and she doesn't have a car' Jeff pointed out.

'But who would have it in for someone like Tina Webb to the extent of setting her up for murder?' said Rebecca.

'As soon as we move forward something else pulls us back' said Jeff. 'And all we're left with are a bunch of possibilities with nothing to tie them together'.

'But if she's not our murderer' said Ollie. 'If something did happen to Clifton after he left her flat then how do we account for the Rohipnol, the knife and the bag of clothes?'

Jeff stared at the mission board with its pictures and its arrows and notes in various different styles of handwriting.

'But who could've helped her?' Rebecca argued behind him. 'The two friends she was with have got alibis for the remainder of that night'.

Andrea Kay hastily made up the bed in her Grandma's spare room. Tina Webb stood numbly at the door.

'There' said Andrea. 'You'll be okay in here'.

'Thank you' said Tina before bursting into tears.

Andrea put her arms round her. 'Hey, it's okay'.

'You know me, Andrea. I'm all gob and dirty talk. I never thought I'd ever go through anything like this'.

'Tina, the police have released you under caution pending further enquiries. That means they don't really think that you did it. And during those enquiries they'll find out for sure that you didn't'.

'But I swear to God I knew nothing about those knives or those clothes. Somebody made sure they could be linked to me but who'd do that to me, Andrea?'

'I don't know, love' said Andrea. 'Are you sure there's nobody in your life who you may have upset in some way?'

'But to the extent that they set me up for murder?'

'I know' said Andrea. 'It does seem a bit far-fetched but I'm clutching at straws trying to find some answers for you'.

'You do believe me, don't you?'

'Of course I do. Do you think I'd invite a murderer to stay in my Grandma's house? I know you didn't do it, Tina. Nobody who knows you could ever believe that you could've done it. We've just got to convince those idiot police of that now'.

'They want to pin it on me'.

'They won't succeed' said Andrea. 'Now I like Ryan your solicitor. He seems to have it all up top'.

'I don't know how I'm going to be able to pay him'.

'You don't have to worry about that' said Andrea. 'I'm covering the cost'.

'No, Andrea … '

' … look, I won't hear any objection from you about it. I've still got some of the money my mother left me and I'm going to use it to get my best mate out of trouble'.

'I'll have to pay you back at some stage'.

'No, you won't. It's a gift. You're innocent and I'm going to help you prove it and whilst Ryan does what he needs to do my Gran says you can stay here as long as you like'.

'Thank you' said Tina. 'Your Gran is letting me stay and I can't thank her enough. I don't think I could've been alone tonight. And I've got to speak to the Welsh dragon tomorrow'.

'We'll do that together' said Andrea. 'Now I think you should try and get some sleep. Gran is downstairs making some tea and I'll bring it up along with a brandy. We'll fix all of this somehow, Tina. I don't know how yet but we'll find a way'.

FIREFLIES EIGHT

After they'd finished for the day, Rebecca decided to give in and go for a drink with Jonathan Freeman.

'So where are you from, Jonathan?' she asked. She liked the way he looked. They'd gone straight from the office to the pub and he needed a shave. She liked that. She liked the way his hair seemed to fall back into a sort of order after he'd run his hands through it too. She also liked that slight gap in his top front teeth and the little dimple in his chin. Should she carry on talking to him or cut straight to the invitation back to her place?

'Portsmouth originally' he answered. 'But I went to university up here and after I qualified I decided to stay. Well there was a girl involved then but we're not seeing each other anymore'.

'There's a lot of people in the city these days from all sorts of places' said Rebecca.

'Yeah, well that's the same everywhere' said Jonathan who tried to keep his voice even. He didn't want to give anything away.

'I meant that was a good thing'.

'Oh so did I' said Jonathan, putting on his best bewildered smile.

'Good' said Rebecca. 'Because anyone else might've been forgiven for thinking you were hinting at some kind of racism'.

'Me? I'm no racist, Rebecca'.

'I'm glad to hear it'.

'I do think that immigration has gone too far though and we need to review it'.

'What kind of immigration? The white Australian barmaid who served us our drinks five minutes ago or the black Somalian with a different culture who just wants a better life for himself and his family?'

'Rebecca, don't try and trap me into saying what I don't want to say'.

'I wasn't trying to. But you'd know if I was'.

'Don't you ever let racial stereotypes get into your thinking at work?'

'I see a crime, Jonathan, not a race'.

'Then that's why you're a great detective'.

'Well recovered. I'm impressed'.

'My Dad used to be a Tory councillor'.

'Used to be?'

'He defected to UKIP about six months ago on the issue of immigration. He thinks its gone way too far'.

'Jonathan, let's get away from politics. Otherwise we won't get through another drink and it's your round'.

'I bought the last one'

'I know. You're such an old-fashioned gentleman'.

Jonathan came back from the bar with the drinks and said 'I really hope you haven't got me all wrong, Rebecca'.

'So do I' said Rebecca who thought he was as sexy as fuck and wanted him there and then. 'I don't want anything serious, Jonathan'.

Jonathan paused in that way men do when they think they've been given a green light. 'Who mentioned anything serious?'

'Drink up'.

Rebecca asked Jonathan back to her place and happily discovered that he was a formidable lover who had more than a few ways to pleasure her. Jonathan loved licking out a woman especially after he'd been in there with his cock. The tastes that were unleashed reminded him that he could never do without sex. He wondered if his Dad ever did this to his Mum. His Mum would no doubt think his Dad was disgusting for even suggesting it. He licked and kissed his way up Rebecca's body, stopping to suck on each of her breasts before turning over and lying beside her. She'd been quick with her orgasm when they fucked and now, as her straight hair fell against his shoulders, he lit a couple of the strong continental cigarettes he liked so much and handed one to her. She took a long, deep drag.

'If you'd have told me this morning when I came into work that I would be having that kind of sex with you before the day was out then I'd have laughed my head off' said Rebecca who was feeling on top of the bloody world for the first time in weeks.

'It was inevitable it was going to happen from that first moment we met in the office'.

'But you didn't know anything about me then?'

'I knew you were giving me a hard-on'.

Rebecca laughed out loud. 'Seriously?'

'Yeah' said Jonathan as he shifted his bum in the bed.

'But you didn't know anything about me. I might've been happily married'.

'That didn't stop me from having it away with the bride at a wedding'.

Rebecca's jaw dropped. 'You dirty bastard'.

'And her mother'.

'You are joking'.

'No, straight up'.

'Well yes I know all about that with you' said Rebecca. 'In fact, I can see you're getting it on again, aren't you?'

'Why don't you slip your hand down there and find out?'

Rebecca slipped her hand under the duvet and sure enough Jonathan was getting another whopper of an erection. She wrapped her fingers lightly round it and stroked it gently.

'I'm not much of a mystery man, Rebecca'.

'Not much?'

'Every gentleman keeps some things secret just like every lady'.

'After the sex we've just had I don't think there's much about me you don't know'.

'I know that you've got beautifully shaped breasts that are just the right size for my hands' said Jonathan as he caressed her breasts with his free hand. He then fingered his way down her body and penetrated her with his finger and started massaging around. 'I know that you're very accommodating down here'.

Rebecca arched her back and gasped. He'd found the place again just like he'd done before and his finger would be wet through when he brought it out.

'God, that feels good' said Rebecca, her head back.

Jonathan began to kiss her breasts and then bite on her erect nipples. She could feel his erection against the top of her leg and she wanted him inside her again. Jonathan brought his finger out and licked it dry as she watched. Then he gently parted her legs and was taking her again.

'You're a dirty job but somebody's got to do you' said Jonathan as he went into the rhythm.

'I'll bet there's a lot of dirt on you, Jonathan' she blurted out between gasps. She wrapped her arms round his neck and then slid her hands go down into the small of his back where she urged him in deeper.

'Me? The only dirt you'll find on me, sweetheart, are the stains I make on your sheets'.

By the time they'd finished the second time Rebecca had lost track of whatever the time was. But somehow she didn't care. It had taken Jonathan to walk into her life and sweep her off her feet to make her admit to herself that her feelings for Jeff Barton were complicated.

'I should never have let this happen, Jonathan'.

'What have you got to be guilty about?'

'Oh nothing. I was just thinking'.

'Don't think. People do too much bloody thinking. Just do is what I say. It felt right to have sex with you and I'm so glad we did. But some people would've still been thinking about it. You know?'

'I know'.

'I've never seen the point' said Jonathan. 'I'm not very English in that way'.

'No, you're not very English at all' said Rebecca. She ran the back of her hand through the hairs on Jonathan's chest. 'You are so open, Jonathan. That's one of the things I really like about you'.

'One of the things?'

'Well okay, that and your big cock'.

'Yeah, he's not a bad size, I'll grant you that'.

'I shouldn't be laughing like this as if I haven't got a care in the world'.

'That's because right at this minute you haven't'.

'Right at this minute?'

'Well I'm aware I'm a poor substitute for the boss'.

Rebecca sat upright. 'What did you say?'

'It's not only women who are perceptive' said Jonathan. 'The whole station know there's something unspoken going on between you and Jeff Barton. To be honest they all wish the two of you would just get on with it'.

Rebecca was mortified to think that everybody had been talking about her and Jeff when there was no her and Jeff to talk about. 'Everybody knows?'

'Pretty much'.

'So what was this all about?'

'Well seeing as I didn't exactly have to drag you here kicking and screaming then why don't you tell me what it's all about?'

'A diversion?'

'Yes, we're adults, Rebecca and we've had fantastic fun. A fun diversion with no strings'.

'It doesn't bother you that I might have feelings for someone else?'

Jonathan shrugged his shoulders. 'It didn't bother me when I was fucking a bride and an hour later her mother when their respective husbands were at the bar'.

'A bride on her wedding day? That's low, Jonathan'.

'Lower than doing it with her mother do you think?'

'I don't know. I'll have to ponder that one'.

'Well don't ponder too much. Too much pondering and thinking is very bad for the spontaneity in the soul'.

'Oh I've been played good and proper'.

'Yes you have' said Jonathan. 'But not by me. I mean, who do you think has been spreading it around the station that you and the boss have got the hots for each other?'

'Tell me?'

'DC Ollie Wright'.

'Ollie?'

'Oh yes'.

'I don't believe it' said Rebecca. 'Ollie is the last person I would think of as a gossip'.

'Well I've only been there five minutes and I can see right through him' said Jonathan. 'He's been putting it around about you and the boss'.

'I can't believe it. Ollie?'

'It's what those bitter and twisted Queen types do'.

'Now you've lost me again?'

'Is that something else you didn't know? Rebecca, Ollie is gay. He's probably hot for Barton which is why he decided to spread his poison. He's jealous of you'.

'Well now you are being ridiculous'.

'Am I?'

'I don't mean about Ollie being gay because I couldn't care less about that' said Rebecca. 'But I would never take him for the nasty vicious Queen that you're making him out to be'.

''Rebecca, all I can tell you is that he's given me nothing but a hard time since I started' said Jonathan. 'He more or less accused me of trying to steal his wallet the other day'.

'You're not serious?'

'Oh yes I am and it's true what they say. You sometimes don't really know those closest to you'.

'I'm sorry to have to do this, Tina' said Paula Jones, the supermarket manageress.

'So that means that I'm not going to like it'.

'Tina, I have to put the interests of the store and the company before anything. That's the only way I can protect all the staff and our customers. Do you understand?'

'No' said Tina who was resenting being held on the Welsh dragon's carpet. After all she'd already been through the last thing she needed was this.

'Your presence here may be disturbing for our customers' said Paula, trying to reason. 'Surely you can see that?'

'No, I can't' Tina countered. 'The responsibility for what happened lies solely with whoever did kill James Clifton and that wasn't me'.

'Well I'm suspending you pending further investigations. I'll be writing to you later today to make the decision formal'.

'No way! On what grounds are you suspending me?'

'For bringing the store into disrepute'.

'That's crap and you know it!'

'Could I ask you not to use bad language, please'.

'Oh well, sorry if I offend but I'm fighting my corner here against a prison cell and I'm just not going to let you put me in that position'.

'You don't have any choice, Tina. My decision has been approved by head office and is final'.

'Because you and head office have decided I'm guilty? What happened to innocent until proven guilty, eh? Or have you and head office decided to write your own laws?'

'I'm very sorry you see it that way'.

'Well that's what it comes down to' said Tina. 'And you know it'.

The door to the office opened and Andrea Kay came in.

'Andrea, it is not appropriate for you to walk into my office like that and in these circumstances'.

'Oh yes it is' said Andrea, firmly. 'I'm the union shop steward for this branch and Tina is one of my members. You shouldn't have even been talking to her officially without consulting me first'.

'Oh I'm sorry but I thought that as the manager I was running the store'.

'You haven't followed correct procedure in terms of industrial relations but we'll deal with that later' said Andrea who knew she'd got the Welsh bitch and from the look on her face so did the Welsh bitch. 'But let's deal with this first'.

'I'm suspending Tina for bringing the store into disrepute'.

'Well I'm sorry you've taken such a reckless decision because you will have to reverse it now'.

'You don't tell me what to do, Andrea'.

'On this occasion I think you'll find I do, Paula'.

Paula Jones was seething. Andrea Kay had got the better of her and she hated it.

'Tina?' said Paula. 'I will consult with head office and then review my earlier decision'.

'No, you'll withdraw it now' said Andrea.

'I'm starting to seriously object to your tone, Andrea'.

'Object to whatever you like but withdraw this nonsense over Tina'.

'Or else?'

'Or else I'll bring this store out on unofficial action if need be'.

'That would be suicide for your career and your position as shop steward'.

'But it would generate an awful lot of negative publicity for the store and you as manager would be in the firing line too. Are you prepared to take that risk?'

'Are you that desperate for a friend?'

'I beg your pardon? Tina would be prepared to do back office duties until the court case is cleared, wouldn't you Tina?'

'Erm, yes, I would' said Tina.

'Oh whatever, okay Tina, there'll be nothing more said on the matter. Consider it closed. Now please get back to work'.

Andrea began to follow Tina out of the office but Paula called her back.

'Let me make one thing very clear' said Paula. 'I do not take threats to my authority lightly. Think again before you try and cross me next time'.

'Excuse me, is that a threat I'm hearing?'

'No, it's a promise' said Paula who was staring Andrea straight in the eyes. 'I'm not one to be crossed'.

Andrea gave a half smile before leaning forward on Paula's desk. 'Well I'm glad we understand each other because I've seen off much better specimens than you so I suggest it's you who needs to watch herself'.

FIREFLIES NINE

Malcolm Barnes hadn't been round the old estate in Wythenshawe where he'd grown up since his parents retired to Scarborough some years previously and he didn't quite know why he was here today. But his cousin Bernie Connolly had insisted.

'I haven't been down here for years' said Malcolm.

'I thought I'd remind you, Malcolm' said Bernie, inhaling deeply on his fat cigar. He knew how uncomfortable his cousin would be. He was from the side of the family who thought they were better than the other side but it's funny how they all come crawling when they need help. 'Now that you're part of the family firm at last'.

Malcolm didn't know how he felt about that particular statement and he wished to God Bernie would put that stupid cigar out because it made him look like the most pathetic of stereotypical gangsters. Malcolm's parents would have a fit if they knew he was even associating with Bernie, let alone doing business with him. Malcolm's mother and Bernie's mother had married two brothers who were very different men. Malcolm's father was the kind of upright citizen who always paid his bills on time and had a good job at the railway. He'd retired on a generous pension. Bernie's father had never had what could be called a career, unless you counted spending three stretches inside a pattern, but he'd been the kind of rogue with a glint in his eye that Bernie's mother had not been able to resist. Although they'd grown up only a street away from each other, Malcolm and Bernie's childhood couldn't have been more different. Malcolm had been brought up in a safe, loving home whilst Bernie had learned very early how to navigate his father's violent tempers until his mother had met local insurance salesman Mike Cooper and left Bernie's father for him. But she left Bernie and his brother Tommy behind and that's a resentment that Bernie will carry with him to the grave. She left them with their violent, drunken abusive father to fend for themselves. Bernie and his brother Tommy had often eaten their meals at Malcolm's place after their mother had gone. Malcolm's mother had tried her best to fill in the gaps in her sister-in-law's mothering skills where Bernie and Tommy were concerned.

But then Bernie had taken it all several steps further. He'd gone into business when he and Malcolm were both still teenagers and Malcolm's parents had forbidden Malcolm from having anything more to do with his cousin. But they had carried on socializing behind their parents' backs until Malcolm stole Tommy Connolly's wife. After that there'd been no contact at all until Malcolm had gone to Bernie for help. There was no doubt though as they walked around that Bernie was held in high regard by the local community, some of whom were coming up and thanking him for sorting this or that out for them.

'So why are we down here, Bernie?'

Bernie led Malcolm round the back of a row of council houses. When they got to the second one along he went up to the back door and knocked. It was opened and they went in. It was dark inside. No lights were on but all the curtains were drawn. There were several of Bernie's henchmen there, all looking the same with their shaved heads and black jackets. A young teenager was tied to a chair in what Malcolm took to be the dining part of the open space on the ground floor of the back of the house. The kitchen was at the other end. The teenager was clearly of Asian origin. He'd been stripped of his trousers. His underpants were visible and he was wearing a white t-shirt under a yellow zip up hooded jacket. His mouth had been stuffed with something and then duck tape had been placed over the top and round the back of his head. The kid looked absolutely terrified. Malcolm wondered what the hell it was all about. It wasn't long before he found out. Bernie pulled up a chair and sat face to face with the kid.

'Now then' he said in a voice almost like a head teacher who'd called a recalcitrant student in for a modern type of bollocking, except there was nothing modern about what was being played out here. 'It's Abid, isn't it?'

The boy nodded rapidly, his terrified eyes widening ever more.

'Well Abid, you see, it's like this. Your father is not playing fair with me. Did you know that?'

Abid shook his head and was trying to speak but he couldn't.

'No, I didn't think so. Well I'm a businessman and round here has been my patch for several years now. I don't appreciate someone trying to muscle in on what's mine, Abid. I don't appreciate it at all and in fact it makes me very angry. You Pakis have got to learn that you can't just walk in and take over everywhere you go but your father has taken things way over the line of acceptability. He's using the Gorton boys to make trouble for me. Those boys can't do any harm to me. Doesn't your father understand that? I could wipe them out like that if I wanted to but that wouldn't be fair, would it. But what I can do is send a message to your father to stop doing business with the Gorton boys. Now I'm sure you want your time with us to be over as quickly as possible. Am I right?'

The kid nodded his head as rapidly as before although this time the room was suddenly filled by the smell of his piss. His pants and the top of the chair were soaking in it and floods of tears were pouring out of his eyes.

'Oh what a fucking dreadful mess' said Bernie, screwing up his face. 'Let's sort you out my friend'.

Bernie clicked his fingers and two of his henchmen moved forward. Abid was struggling to break free as each one took one of his legs in their big, firm hands.

'Tell your father to take this as a warning, Abid'.

Abid's screams were muffled as the two henchmen broke Abid's legs. The sound of Abid's bones breaking made even Bernie flinch and Malcolm stood by and watched a teenage boy having his legs broken. He might as well have done it himself. How had life turned out this way? How had he got himself into such a fucking mess?

'Don't worry, son' said Bernie to Abid who was clearly in excruciating pain. 'We'll make sure you get home safe and sound. But don't forget to give the message to your father'.

Bernie then walked out of the house. Malcolm followed him. Then Bernie stopped and turned. 'Listen, cousin, when you came to me for help you knocked on my door and you entered my world according to my rules. I've no time for squeamish so-called men who can't get anything done because the world has to be pretty and neat and tidy or they can't handle it. Don't forget that I'm only able to help you get out of the shit you're in because of the way I do my business and I shouldn't even be doing that after what you and that slut of a wife of yours did to my brother Tommy'.

'We've already paid a bloody high price for that, Bernie'.

'So you have. I just needed to have that conversation with you to make sure. You are family after all'.

Later that day Bernie leaned back in his swivel chair at his desk in the office room of the fully detached house in the quintessential Cheshire set town of Knutsford when he noticed out of the window Malcolm pulling up in his car. Bernie's Fillipino wife Linda showed Malcolm in. They got down to business straight away. Malcolm in particular didn't want to waste any time.

'So once this latest financial transaction goes through, Bernie, you'll control twenty-five percent of Barnes Financial Services' said Malcolm.

'And a hundred percent of it used to be yours, Malcolm. How does that make you feel?'

'I'm relieved and grateful to you, Bernie, that the company has received a much needed cash injection and you've saved the day for me' said Malcolm who was pissed off by the way Bernie had rubbed his nose in it with that. It was true that his business had been failing and had fallen perilously close to the finishing line. He'd turned to Bernie because he'd run out of legitimate sources of finance.

'Good because I do like all my business partners to be happy with our respective arrangements'.

'I'm sure you do, Bernie, but like I've said before, I'm grateful for the way you've helped me get out of trouble'.

'Blood is thicker than water, Malcolm, and you are family after all'.

'That's true' said Malcolm who was under no illusions. Bernie was never going to leave him alone. He may have twenty-five percent of the shares but Malcolm wouldn't be able to refuse if Bernie wanted to use the company for his own purposes.

'I like doing business man to man, Malcolm' said Bernie. 'That's why I try and keep women out of my business affairs as much as I can. Men and women doing business together is like opening up a Pandora's box of potential sexual problems. Do you know what I mean? Well of course you do. That's how you managed to steal Kim off my brother'.

'Bernie, Kim and I fell in love. It was nothing personal against Tommy'.

'I know that' said Bernie. 'I mean you can't help who you fall in love with now can you, Malcolm?'

'So why do you keep throwing it at me?'

'Because Tommy did away with himself because of all the hurt you and Kim caused him'.

'Yes, I know and I've said sorry time and time again but …'

' … but nothing, Malcolm. Tommy is gone and I miss him, that's all. I like to try and keep him alive by talking about him as if he's still here. Do you know what I mean?'

'I do that with Kim sometimes' said Malcolm who at one stage didn't think he'd ever be able to get over the loss of his dear wife on their wedding night.

'I'm sure you do, Malcolm. I'm sure you do'.

'Bernie, changing the subject if you will, but what do you expect from me on a day-to-day basis with regard to running the business? You've never really said'.

'Well Malcolm, it's like this' Bernie began, loving every minute of Malcolm's barely concealed anxiety. 'You built up a highly successful enterprise from scratch and I admire you for that, I really do. But you went wrong somewhere and I'm not one of those people who blame the government for everything. Now it may surprise you to hear that but it's true. Sometimes we as citizens have to take responsibility for our own actions'.

Malcolm could've laughed at what he was hearing. What a load of old bollocks.

'So, I'll keep an eye on things from a distance' Bernie went on. 'I'll be looking at the books from time to time and before we go on I'd just like to get some figures straight with you because this morning I've completed the purchase of all your debts, both what you owe and what is owed to you'.

Malcolm was suddenly breathless. He hadn't seen that one coming at all and his accountant had mentioned nothing. What the fuck did this mean?

'Your accountant is a very helpful man' Bernie went on. 'He gave me and my team access to anything about the company accounts that we thought was needed. I told him not to say anything to you until I'd looked to see if there was anything I could do. I mean, I didn't want to build your hopes up only to have to piss on them when push came to shove. But surprisingly enough, they weren't as bad as I thought they might be so I thought, why not? Let Malcolm have a real breather from all that worrying he's been doing. It does mean of course that, with the added investment, I now control just over ninety-one percent of Barnes Financial Services. That's right, Malcolm. I'm the majority shareholder now and you're an employee. Now, shall we work out a salary package for you? It'll have to be low to start with of course until the business is truly back on its feet again'.

Malcolm felt sick. He'd been well and truly played and now everything he'd ever worked for over the last twenty years had gone. It had been taken out of his hands by this jumped up gangster who thought he was Cheshire's answer to fucking Al Capone. And there was absolutely nothing he could do about it.

'Don't look so glum, Malcolm' said Bernie. 'Worse things could've happened. You might've had to join the ranks of the unemployed if I hadn't have stepped in when you asked me. I'd say you've come out of this pretty well and of course, you can always let me buy your remaining shares at a heavily discounted price?'

'You've stabbed me in the back' said Malcolm as calmly as he could, even though inside his soul was raging.

'No, I haven't, I've saved you and your business'.

'You took advantage of the fact that I was vulnerable and you stabbed me in the back'.

'Be careful what you're saying, Malcolm'.

'I've put everything I had and more into that business and you can't just come along and take it away from me'.

'I think that's just what I have done, Malcolm'.

'But it's not fair!'

'Neither was it fair when you dumped my sister for Kim' said Bernie. 'Life has been very hard for her since then but life has a way of providing opportunities for the wronged to get justice in the end. Don't you think so, Malcolm?'

'But really was stealing my business from me all about revenge for what happened between me and your sister?'

'I value my little sister's happiness greatly, Malcolm'.

'You're enjoying this' Malcolm sneered.

'Too right I am. And whilst we're on the subject of payback, I loved your mother like she was my own and she made me feel like I was another son. But I wasn't as clever as you at school and when I decided to look into other ways of getting ahead in life she cut me off like I was on the end of a piece of string. I've never forgotten nor forgiven, Malcolm, and I never will. Now I've been waiting for an opportunity to settle the score for my side of the family and you came along and handed it to me on a golden plate'.

'My wife is dead!'

'I know that'.

'She was murdered!'

'I know that too' said Bernie.

'Well don't you think I've suffered enough?'

'It's so hard to measure something like suffering, Malcolm, especially when the emotional health and well-being of my sister are at stake. It's called family, Malcolm. Your side of our family won't be familiar with the concept'.

'You won't get away with it!' roared Malcolm.

'And what are you going to do about it, Malcolm? I mean, do you seriously believe you can ever get one over on me?'

' I'll fucking have you!'

'Now I'm a patient man, Malcolm, but watch your tongue or you may end up with it cut off and I mean literally. You know what I'm capable of. Now you just run along home and pour yourself a large drink. Sit down, relax, take in what's happened to you and contemplate your future. Oh and remember me to your mother. I notice you bought her and Uncle Bill a lovely looking place in Scarborough. I do hope it's a safe area. You hear such stories about old people in their homes these days. It makes me wonder what the world is coming to'.

FIREFLIES TEN

'Look, I told Tina that the best way to deal with her current problems is to adopt a cheerful attitude' said Paula Jones who was being confronted by Andrea Kay after Tina Webb had got upset about what Paula had said to her.

'And is that what you'll say to her when she gets sent down?'

'A positive attitude with a cheerful smile goes a long way, Andrea'.

'Paula, you can't just clear all the darkness out of your life by putting on a bloody smile!'.

'I also told her that if she looks like a guilty person she'll be regarded as a guilty person'.

'Paula, for God's sake! She's been accused of a murder she didn't commit'.

'You know that for sure?'

'Yes, because I know my friend and I stand by her'.

'Well that's very ... touching of you'.

Andrea wanted to punch Paula savagely and break every fucking bone in her Carol Smilie face. 'Words fail me'.

'I hope so because you've said quite enough already' said Paula. 'It's my own son's stag night this weekend. How do I know your friend who you're so heroically supporting isn't targeting stag parties for some evil, twisted reason? I shall be nervous on Saturday night until I know Piers is safely back at home'.

'Oh for God's sake, Paula! What you're saying is slanderous'.

'But it may be true'

'Well don't say it again unless you've got a very good solicitor because I'll make sure Tina sues you for every last penny you've got'.

Jeff Barton and Rebecca Stockton were interviewing James Clifton's fiancée Sophie Cooper in her West Didsbury flat. It was on the first floor of a three storey grand old Victorian villa that characterized much of the houses in the immediate district. They were all set back from the road and trees lined the pavements beyond the front yards that were nearly all given over to residents' parking. Jeff parked the car down the side of the house so that he and Rebecca could take a view of the whole property before going in.

They hadn't said much to each other on the drive down from the station. There was a tense, heavy atmosphere between them. Rebecca was convinced that Jeff would know about her feelings for him from what Jonathan had said was going round the squad. It must've got back to him. It stood to reason. And now that she'd slept with Jonathan it mattered to Rebecca more than ever that Jeff didn't know that little piece of the story. But she was going to say her piece when she caught up with Ollie Wright. Oh yes, he wouldn't know what had hit him.

Sophie Cooper's flat was furnished rather traditionally which surprised both Jeff and Rebecca. A lot of dark greens, dark browns, with flashes of ivory and cream to lighten the mood here and there.

'How long have you had this place, Sophie?' Jeff asked. There was something about her he recognized and he was trying his damndest to recall what it was.

Sophie cleared her throat. She was perched on the edge of the sofa playing constantly with a paper tissue in her hand. She wasn't wearing any make-up and her hair hung lifelessly just on the top of her shoulders which were hunched forward.

'James and I bought it last year' she answered in a quiet voice.

'And were you happy here?'

'Yes' she said, without hesitation. 'It's convenient for town and for my work at the airport. James also had a more or less straight run to the BBC studios at Salford Quays. It only took him ten minutes to get to work'.

'It must be hard for you, Sophie' said Rebecca who could see the darkness in Sophie's eyes. 'Haven't you got anybody who can come and be with you?'

'I prefer to be on my own to be honest' she revealed. 'There's only me and my brother and he's great but I'm better off coming to terms with things on my own. I've got my friends too of course who've all rallied round. Anyway, I hear you got the bitch who murdered my James?'

'We've cautioned Tina Webb, Sophie, pending further enquiries' said Jeff. 'Do you know her?'

'No, of course I don't. Why would I?'

'I'm just asking, Sophie. The investigation is still ongoing'.

'Why is it? I know she did it for a fact'.

'But you don't know that, Sophie' said Jeff. 'How could you know?'

'I just know' she said, tearfully. 'I just know'.

'Sophie, there has to be hard evidence to secure a conviction'.

'I don't understand? If you think she did it then why the hesitation?'

'We need to build a strong enough case that will have a chance of succeeding' said Jeff. 'That's why'.

'How would you describe your relationship with James, Sophie?' asked Rebecca.

'I beg your pardon?'

'Well were you happy? Were there any problems of any kind?'

'How dare you! No, we didn't have any problems. We were engaged and we were going to get married. Oh I suppose you've been talking to his so-called mates? Like Alan Travers and his witch of a girlfriend Lucy? They all hated me. And do you know why? Because I was better than any of them'.

Jeff and Rebecca exchanged a look.

'So you didn't get on with any of his friends?' asked Jeff.

'No, they didn't get on with me' Sophie insisted. 'I was letting them into my world with James. They were visitors. They should've behaved appropriately'.

'How do you mean?'

'Well they were always talking about things they'd done in the past before I met James' said Sophie. 'I hated it. I wanted the day we met to be his year zero and for him to believe that nothing else mattered before I came along. But he couldn't go along with my wishes. He couldn't break those ties with that lot for me'.

'But why would you want him to?'

'I was his fiancée. I shouldn't have had to give a reason. He should've just done whatever I wanted him to do'.

'Even if he felt it was unreasonable?'

'Whatever he felt about it' said Sophie. 'The expression of my wishes should've been enough'.

Fuck's sake, thought Rebecca. If she'd been a man she'd have run a million miles from Sophie at the earliest opportunity. Talk about psycho.

'Sophie' said Rebecca. 'Tina Webb claims that James wanted her to perform certain sexual acts and she refused. That's when he lost his temper and hit her'.

'Did he ever hit you, Sophie?' asked Jeff.

'Look, James was highly sexed' Sophie admitted, her eyes darting all around her as if revealing the secret would somehow bring James back to life. 'He needed it all the time'.

'And if you refused or didn't want to?'

Sophie tucked her hair behind her ears. 'Then sometimes he'd lose it a bit. Okay? Is that what you wanted to here?'

'So he did hit you?' Jeff pursued.

Sophie nodded her head in reply. 'It was never hard. Just a slap'.

'How often?' asked Rebecca.

'Once a month' said Sophie. 'Sometimes it was more than that. And you see, I don't always do there and back flights. I go away for two or three days night stopping and I knew he'd find sex elsewhere whilst I was gone'.

'And that didn't bother you?'

'I knew what he needed'.

'That doesn't make it right, Sophie'.

'Look, the man is dead! And even if he slapped me a few times he didn't deserve to die the way he did. So don't give me that sanctimonious look of pity and scorn. You're not me and I'm glad I'm not you'.

'Sophie … '

' … oh and how do you keep a man? You should be able to tell me seeing as you sit there looking like you wrote the fucking book on it!'

'Sophie, DS Stockton was only concerned for you' said Jeff. 'There's no need for you to speak to her like that'.

'Yeah, well it's how I feel so she should take responsibility for it because it's her fault'.

'Sophie, how long had you known about James cheating on you?' Jeff asked.

'He blurted it out in a row we had one night after I'd been away' Sophie revealed. 'We'd only been together a couple of months'.

'But what did you feel about the loss of trust?'

'Look, I get that men can have sex and it means nothing more than that. I also knew how seductive the James Clifton charm could be and how he loved to flirt. God knows he was a bloody attractive man but that's not to say I was never tempted to stray myself'.

'And did you ever?'

'No, I didn't' said Sophie. 'But I was tempted on a couple of occasions when someone took a shine to me and sex with an attractive man in some hotel room in Newcastle or wherever seemed like something I could enjoy and get away with. But I never gave in. It wasn't for any moral reasons. I just didn't because I would've known and I would've had to live with it. But as far as James was concerned I was glad that somebody else took the strain sometimes if I'm honest. He was very particular about what he wanted. He and I had a good and a varied sex life but when we experimented with different things it was always at his instigation and he didn't like it if I was reluctant to try something new. So yes, I could see that if he did go to the effort of picking someone up who didn't go along with his sexual intentions then it would be a problem for him'.

'Are you sure he never got more violent than the occasional slap, Sophie?'

'Yes, of course I'm sure' said Sophie, her heart hardening to the two officers. 'Look, are you trying to paint my fiancé as someone who was fond of using his fists for a reason? Are you trying to get this Tina Webb off on some self-defence shit?'

'No, not at all, Sophie' said Jeff who was beginning to feel like Sophie Cooper was lying through her perfectly whitened teeth. He was also bothered by the notion that he probably knew more about Sophie Cooper than his memory would first let on. There was something vaguely familiar about her and the more she talked the more he felt it. 'Like we said before, we just need to draw an accurate overall picture'.

'So Sophie Cooper was in an abusive relationship with our murder victim' said Rebecca in the car on the way back to the station. 'And she was too stupid to tell him to fuck off'.

'That's a bit harsh, isn't it Becky?'

'Well I just don't get it with women like that, sir' said Rebecca. 'I'm sorry but I just don't understand why an attractive young woman like Sophie Cooper would even contemplate marrying a man who slapped her when she didn't want to have sex, or worse, the kind of sex he wanted. I mean, is this not the twenty-first century? Have we not arrived at a time when women don't have to do what their men try to insist upon?'

'Well like you I hope we have arrived at that place and we as police officers are there to enforce it' said Jeff. 'But domestic violence is one of the hardest things to understand in our line of work. The act itself is wrong and I could no more hit a woman than I could hit Toby'.

'You think that smacking a child is wrong?'

'Yes I do' said Jeff. 'A smack is a physical assault and because you're perpetrating it against a defenceless child is even worse than if you were doing it against an adult. They say it's something boys get from their fathers but I know that my Dad hit my Mum and me and my brother and sister on occasions and yet I haven't turned into the same kind of man. I made a decision that I wouldn't do. So where I have a problem is when people, men and women, claim it's because they grew up with domestic violence. Surely they should take responsibility for their own lives and know that it's wrong'.

'I agree' said Rebecca. 'But that's because you're strong and those others are weak'.

'I suppose I must be strong to have got through the last few months'.

'That's rare for you'.

'What is?'

'You giving yourself some credit' said Rebecca. She blushed. She wished it was Jeff she was slipping under the duvet with. Jonathan knew how to make a girl happy alright but it was Jeff who her soul was crying out for.

'Well' said Jeff. He was getting self-conscious now. 'Let's get back to the case'.

'I do kind of see now though that Sophie Cooper seems like she'd have been an absolute nightmare to have a relationship with'.

'She most certainly does' said Jeff. 'Intense isn't strong enough a word'.

'But that doesn't give James Clifton the right to hit her'.

'I want a complete picture of Sophie Cooper's life. I want to know if she's been involved in any abusive relationships before. In fact I want to know about all her previous relationships'.

'She did seem to be a little bit too insistent about how happy she and Clifton were' said Rebecca.

'I know her from somewhere' said Jeff.

'Really?'

'It's been bugging me since her name was first mentioned' said Jeff. 'Damn it, I wish I could remember'.

FIREFLIES ELEVEN

'So why are Lancashire CID letting us do this?' asked Rebecca as Jeff drove them up the M61 towards Preston.

'Short of manpower, they want to make a point of some kind. It could be anybody's guess'.

'And meanwhile we're going way out of our jurisdiction'.

'Sit back and enjoy the scenery, DS Stockton' said Jeff. 'We don't get a ride out like this very often'.

'Did you remember what you thought you recognized about Sophie Cooper?'

'No' said Jeff 'And it's really starting to annoy me now because I know there's something'.

'Changing the subject completely, have you thought about hiring that guy Brendan as your nanny?'

'Well as a matter of fact, yes' said Jeff. 'I've got his number off our Lewis and I'm going to call him. If his references check out and Toby likes him then I'll give him a trial'.

'I think that's a good idea'.

'Well we'll see'.

'Jeff?'

'Yeah?'

'I've heard that … well I've heard that someone is spreading talk back at the station'.

'Who and about what exactly?'

Rebecca took a deep breath before continuing. 'Ollie Wright has been spreading stuff about you and me'.

'What? Ollie? What's he been saying?'

'That we've got the eye for each other but we're repressing it'.

'And who told you this?'

'Jonathan'.

'Oh' said Jeff. 'Classic'.

'Why do you say that?'

'Well Jonathan is stirring things because he's jealous of our friendship' said Jeff. 'And for some reason he's using Ollie to drive his wedge. And there was me thinking we always worked with grown- ups'.

'But what about Ollie? Isn't he really the villain here?'

'Becky, were you listening just then? I believe that Jonathan is lying because he's jealous of our friendship and he's using Ollie for some unfathomable reason to make himself look good. I mean, come on Becky, do you really think that Ollie Wright would spread gossip about his two senior officers especially when we're on such good terms with each other?'

'Well I agree it's uncharacteristic' said Rebecca. 'And I was surprised. But Jonathan insists it's him'.

'No, I just don't buy it' said Jeff. 'Although I'm not surprised there may be talk about us. I mean, even in this day and age a man and woman can't be colleagues and friends without small minds reading something sordid into it'.

'Wait a minute? Are you saying that if something was going on between us it would be sordid?'

'No, Rebecca, I'm not saying that at all' said Jeff, wearily. 'I'm just making a general comment about people and the way they behave. I get the feeling that whatever I say in this conversation is going to land me in it one way or another'.

'What's that supposed to mean?'

'Look, will you just lighten up?'

'You meant something by it, Jeff'.

'It's just words I threw out'.

'Oh give me strength'.

'What did you say?'

'Nothing. Well are you going to speak to Ollie Wright about it?'

'No, because I don't believe he's guilty of anything and I do believe that the more you protest that something isn't true the more people will believe that it is'.

'Jonathan told me that Ollie is gay too'.

'Well hold the front page! Some of the officers of the Greater Manchester police force are gay? Now that will be news. I must tell my brother Lewis. He's gay, you know? He'll be thrilled to hear that'.

Despite herself Rebecca couldn't help laughing.

'There you are' said Jeff. 'The old Rebecca who laughs with me is back. I'd missed her. I'd beware of that jealous new boyfriend of yours though'.

'He's not my boyfriend, Jeff'.

'Ah, so it's just about sex'.

'Do you mind?' Rebecca exclaimed.

'No' said Jeff. 'What you do in your personal life is none of my business, Rebecca'.

Fred and Sue Clifton sat on their sofa in the living room of their three-storey Victorian house just off the main A6 north of Preston city centre. It was a relatively quiet street considering its proximity to the main road, thought Jeff. The couple were holding hands. They both looked rocked by grief. Their eyes were moist and there was a grey pallor all around them.

'James was our eldest son' said Sue Clifton. 'We have a younger son and two daughters. It's not just that he's dead but it was the way … I'm sorry'.

Jeff leaned forward in the chair he was sitting in beside Sue Clifton. 'It's okay. We understand. We're very sorry for your loss, Mr and Mrs. Clifton, and we're doing everything we can to catch whoever was responsible'.

'Mr. and Mrs. Clifton, we have to ask' said Rebecca.

'If our son had any enemies who hated him enough to kill him?' asked Fred Clifton.

'Yes, sir' said Rebecca.

'No' he said as emphatically as he could give considering how he was feeling. 'James was a good, hard working lad. We were proud that he was our son. We were proud of the way he'd turned out. Every time we watched North West tonight on the BBC we knew he was behind the scenes somewhere looking after things. He was a credit to us'.

'He was living the dream as they say nowadays' said Sue Clifton. 'He'd always wanted to work in television but behind the scenes. He'd never wanted to present or act or do anything in front of the cameras. We're just working class folk but our James took us into a whole different world with some of his stories'.

'So nobody had a grudge against him as far as you knew' said Rebecca.

'No' said Fred. 'And we were close to James like we are to all our children. We speak to them all at some point every day'.

'Now we're going to miss those calls from James' said Sue. 'It just isn't fair and I tell you this. I think you should look close to home for answers'.

'How do you mean, Mrs. Clifton?' asked Jeff.

'His fiancée Sophie set herself against our family as soon as she got together with James. She decided that she didn't like us even before we'd met'.

'We tried ringing Sophie to see if she was okay after we'd been told what had happened to James' Fred went on. 'So did our daughter Carol. We just wanted to see if she was okay and if she needed company. But Sophie was so abrupt and downright rude that we haven't rung again because in the circumstances we just don't need it. Now she's causing bother over the funeral. We want him buried up here naturally where we can tend the grave and take care of it. But she's tried to get him buried near to her and we've once again had to put our foot down'.

'How do you mean once again?'

'Well' said Sue. 'When they started planning the wedding, or rather when Sophie started planning the wedding, she said it was going to be a cocktail reception in some swanky Manchester bar and that no kids would be invited. Well that was a direct hit against our family because we've got five grandchildren and James has always been close to his nieces and nephews. It really hurt that she was trying to exclude them from the wedding. She wasn't even planning to ask one of them to be a bridesmaid or a page boy'.

'And did that get resolved?' asked Rebecca.

'Only after James insisted that he wanted his whole family at the wedding' said Sue.

'And she didn't speak to him for days after that just because he wouldn't let her have her own way for once' said Fred. 'She can sulk for England that one'.

'I asked James a couple of times if he really wanted to spend the rest of his life with someone who behaved like that' Sue added. 'But he said he was in love with her so what could he do? Then there's the family connection. Talk about unfortunate'.

'Why, Mrs. Clifton?' asked Rebecca. 'What is the family connection?'

'Well don't you know? I thought that would be one of the reasons why you were here? Sophie Cooper's brother is one of the most notorious gangsters in Manchester'.

'What's her brother's name, Mrs. Clifton?' asked Jeff.

'Bernie Connelly! Have we got to tell you your job? Sophie has only got the name of Cooper because she and her brother had different fathers. Do you really not know any of this?'

'Alright' said Jeff as he tried to keep his voice level. His emotions were running high. Since he knew exactly why the name of Sophie Cooper had meant something to him he'd been on a painful journey into both his professional and personal past. 'Was there no connection between Cooper and Connelly evident when we were digging?'

'Well to be fair, sir' said Jonathan Freeman. 'I can't let DC Wright take the rap for this'.

'There's no rap to be taken Jonathan' said Jeff. 'I knew that I recognized the name of Sophie Cooper and I should've made the connection there and bloody then. I just want to know why it wasn't clear anywhere else'.

'Well the link wasn't obvious because of the difference in surname, sir' Jonathan went on. 'And I looked it over twice and I'm sure DC Wright would've got there in time if I'd passed on the complete information. If anybody is to blame, sir, it's me'.

Ollie turned and looked at Freeman completely unable to believe he'd just had such a measure of support from him. There'd be something behind it though. He'd got to know his devious ways well enough to be certain of that.

'Well look, I'm not interested in playing the accusation game' said Jeff. 'But you can bet your life that Bernie Connelly will have his dirty little fingers all over this in some way. So, Ollie, tell everybody about him'.

Ollie stood up and took up the space left for him by Jeff at the mission board. He'd spent the last hour researching Bernie Connelly since the boss rang him from Preston.

'Ladies and gentlemen this is complicated so if I could please have your full attention' said Ollie. He pointed to the picture he'd just stuck to the board. 'Let's start with Bernie Connelly. Now, as many of you will know we've been trying to bring him down for years. Under the disguise of his legitimate business, Connelly Security, who provide security guards to whoever wants them, we suspect that he runs a series of protection rackets across the city in a distinctly Mafiosi style. His latest offensive is against a gang of British men of Pakistani descent who want to muscle in on Connelly's territory. We strongly suspect that he arranged to have the son of one of the Pakistani leaders abducted as an opener in a turf war. The fifteen-year old boy was returned to his family with both his legs broken'.

'How do we know about the Pakistani boy?'

'Because the organized crime unit have an informant in Connelly's organization, sir' Ollie revealed. 'It's his former brother-in-law Malcolm Barnes'.

'His former brother-in-law?' Rebecca questioned.

'Yes, ma'am' Ollie confirmed. He pinned some more pictures to the board and pointed at them whilst he talked. 'Connelly was the son of Ted and mother Marie. Marie left the drunken, abusive Ted to move in with her lover Mike Cooper but didn't take Bernie and his brother Tommy with her. She left them with their father. She and Mike Cooper had a daughter called Sophie. Both Marie and Mike Cooper are now dead. Sophie was once engaged to an old family friend called Malcolm Barnes who until recently owned Barnes financial services. But shortly before the wedding he dumped Sophie and went off with the wife of Bernie's brother Tommy Connelly'

'So splitting the family two ways' said Rebecca.

'Oh but there's more, ma'am' said Ollie. 'Tommy's wife was called Kim Connelly and shortly after she left him Tommy Connelly killed himself. Then on the wedding night of Malcolm and Kim Barnes three years ago, Kim was murdered in their suite at the Manchester Hilton whilst Malcolm was outside having a cigarette. And that's a murder that remains unsolved'.

'Ollie, was Malcolm Barnes on his stag night by any chance when he met Kim?' Rebecca wanted to know.

'By chance he was, ma'am' said Ollie. 'The other detail worthy of note is that Malcolm Barnes recently relinquished ownership of his financial services company to Bernie Connelly. But you might call it a hostile takeover. Barnes felt like he'd been swindled by Connelly out of his own company'.

'Revenge for Barnes dumping Sophie three years ago?' Rebecca suggested.

'I think so, ma'am' said Ollie. 'And Barnes has now turned on Connelly because he resents him taking his company off him. We also believe that Connelly runs a number of prostitutes in the city based in some of the major hotels. The organized crime unit are pinning all their current hopes on Malcolm Barnes providing enough information for them to be able to sweep on Connelly and bring him down once and for all.

FIREFLIES TWELVE

'Okay' said Jeff. 'Let me tell you why Bernie Connelly is significant to me. Andy Kirkpatrick was a dedicated and excellent police officer. He was also my friend. We were also professional partners until he moved over to the organized crime unit a year before he died'.

'How did he die, sir?' asked Rebecca.

'It'll be five years ago next February' Jeff recalled. 'He was sitting in his car on a surveillance operation when someone walked up and shot him. It was a classic professional hit and he was part of the investigating team trying to penetrate the iron curtain around Bernie Connelly. Andy was godfather to my son Toby. So now you know what nailing Connelly means to me'.

'Not meaning to sound insensitive, sir, but how do you know it was Bernie Connelly who ordered the hit on Andy Kirkpatrick?' asked Rebecca.

'Well I don't in terms of cold, hard facts' said Jeff. 'But Andy was getting close, very close, to getting enough information on Connelly to nail him and that's what got him killed'.

'What happened to the enquiries on the Kim Barnes murder case?' asked Rebecca.

'Well I wasn't on the investigation team but my understanding is that they couldn't find anything that could point to one individual having been the killer' said Jeff. 'On the one hand they had the husband Malcolm Barnes who was distraught as you can imagine but had no reason for killing his wife, especially not in such a brutal way. Then they had Sophie Cooper, the wronged woman who had every motive but there was no evidence linking her to the crime. All they had was a piece of CCTV showing what looked like a woman entering the hotel just before the time of the incident and leaving a few minutes later having spoken to nobody but looking like she knew where she was going'.

'How did they know it was a woman, sir?' Ollie wanted to know.

'Well they could tell by the shape of the figure even though she was wearing a floor length black coat, massive black sunglasses and a black hat with a large rim round it that almost shadowed her entire face. They put the image out everywhere but nobody came forward with any identification. They must've interviewed getting on for a hundred people during that investigation and nothing. Of course they knew that Bernie Connolly and anyone associated with him would be hard nuts to try and crack open but even so they tried but got nowhere. Eventually they just had to close the file and hand it over to the cold case review team for them to deal with when they saw fit. Like I said I wasn't on that original investigation team but I knew well the senior officers who were'.

'But the interest for us now is in what connection that crime may have with this current investigation' said Ollie. 'Some of the people involved in this case were also involved in the Hilton murder. Was it made certain that the image on the CCTV from the Manchester Hilton was not that of Sophie Cooper, sir?'

'Yes, if I remember correctly, Ollie, the woman in the image was shorter than Sophie Cooper and, shall we say, wider?'

Ollie smiled. 'I get it, sir. But I do think there's something for us to find here. I've gone through the statements from the Mayfair hotel staff and I can detect that something is happening at the hotel that they don't want to talk about, at least not to the police'.

'But what?' asked Rebecca.

'Well could it be that Bernie Connolly's hotel prostitute ring includes the Mayfair?' said Jeff.

'And if it does then did James Clifton end up knowing too much?' Rebecca speculated.

'It's not inconceivable' said Jeff. 'But now I want to bring Sophie Cooper in. I'm just not prepared to believe that there's no connection between her brother and all of this. The new wife of her ex-fiance is murdered. Her current fiancé is murdered. Both were unfaithful to her and we can see how vengeful she could be. There's a link here and we're going to find it'.

'I'll see to that, sir' said Rebecca who then left the squad room. Jeff then asked Ollie Wright to join him in his office.

'Ollie, have you heard any rumours about me?' Jeff asked.

'Rumours? To do with what, sir?'

'Well to do with my relationship with DS Stockton?'

'No, sir' said Ollie. 'I honestly haven't heard anything to do with that, sir'.

Jeff believed him. 'So you wouldn't know if DS Stockton and I are being talked about as if we're involved in something more than just friendship?'

'No, sir' said Ollie. 'I haven't heard anything like that'.

'Well it isn't true anyway just for the record' said Jeff. 'But thanks for answering my questions. And Ollie, is everything okay between you and Jonathan Freeman?'

Jeff noted the look on Ollie's face that told him everything. 'He does his job, sir, and I do mine. But I don't think we'll ever be best friends'.

'Why do you think that is?'

'You'd have to ask him, sir' said Ollie. 'Maybe it's just one of those things. You can't get on with everybody'.

'I don't know why you've brought me in here!' snapped Sophie Cooper. 'You're behaving as if I'm some kind of criminal when it's that cow you let go who's the murderer'.

Jeff and Rebecca sat down on the opposite side of the table from Sophie.

'We just need to ask you a few more questions' said Jeff calmly and in complete contrast to the aggressive tone of Sophie. 'You do like to get your own way, don't you Sophie?'

'So? Is that a crime all of a sudden? It wouldn't surprise me. I was only reading in the Daily Mail the other day … '

' … yes, well I'm sure it was interesting but has no relevance to this case'.

'So what do you want then because I've got a funeral to arrange in case you'd forgotten'.

'Isn't that for James Clifton's parents to see to?' Rebecca questioned.

Sophie looked at Rebecca as if she'd just stepped in her. 'I don't do compromise'.

'Whether they like it or not?'

'I've just lost my fiancé! Doesn't anybody care about me and my feelings or is it just all about them?'

'They've just lost their son'.

'So?'

'Well do you not have any respect for what they want?'

Sophie shook her hair and crossed her legs. 'No is the short answer to that'.

'Why not?'

'Because I don't see why I should have to. James was my fiancé. He belonged to me as soon as he put that engagement ring on my finger and from then on as far as I'm concerned his family were completely out of the picture with no right to any piece of him at all'.

'Phew' said Rebecca.

'Well you did ask and I'm a passionate person when it comes to the truth' said Sophie. 'Don't ask the questions if you can't handle the answers, sweetheart'.

'It must've hurt when Malcolm Barnes ended his relationship with you for another woman?' said Jeff.

'How do you know about that?'

'It's how I remembered you'.

Sophie looked into Jeff's face for a moment. 'You weren't on the case. I don't remember you?'

'No, I wasn't on the case but I knew people who were'.

'Well they never found the killer of that evil bitch Kim so what makes you think you'll do a better job of it this time?'

'Why don't you just answer the question please, Miss Cooper?' said Rebecca.

'Yes it fucking hurt like crazy when Malcolm dumped me for that cow! And yes I wanted to kill her but somebody beat me to it. Alright? Satisfied now?'

'You seem to store a lot of anger inside yourself, Miss Cooper' said Rebecca.

'Well I've had a lot in my life to be angry about' said Sophie. 'I lost both my parents when I was young. I lost one fiancé because he dumped me for someone else and I lost another because of a murdering bitch'.

'James Clifton was unfaithful to you, wasn't he?'

'You seem to know what you're talking about. Who am I to argue?'

'Miss Cooper, was James Clifton unfaithful to you or not!'

'Yes he was! And I hated him for it. But you already know that I didn't kill him, that I couldn't have killed him because I was hundreds of miles away, so why are you going for me like this? Don't you think I've been through enough?'

'Were you and James Clifton on the verge of splitting up because of his infidelity, Miss Cooper?'

'No!' Sophie claimed emphatically. 'Whoever told you that is a liar!'

'How's your brother Bernie Connolly, Miss Cooper?' asked Jeff.

'Oh so now I see. You're trying to get to Bernie through me? You really are pathetic'.

'I just wanted to know how he was, Miss Cooper' said Jeff with a sweep of his open hands. 'No law against that'.

Sophie stood up. 'You have no basis on which to keep me here so I'm going' she said. 'And if you want to know how my brother is then why don't you just go and ask him?'

'I think we probably will' said Jeff. 'In the meantime please pass on my regards'.

'And whilst you're at it get that bitch Tina Webb behind bars where she belongs' said Sophie. 'She murdered my fiancé and instead of making sure justice is served you choose to hound me and my brother. Well it didn't work last time and it won't work this time either'.

Down on the bus station at Mersey square in Stockport was a fish and chip place that really stretched it to call itself a restaurant. Sharon Bellfield found it without any problem. She just had to follow the smell of vinegar and the steady stream of life's unfortunates who saw it as the place to be.

When her boss had given her this assignment she couldn't have had any idea that it would take her into the kind of places that she'd spent her life trying to get out of. Sharon was no snob but as she sat there with a mug of steaming hot liquid they had the nerve to call tea even though the bag had probably been used at least ten times, she couldn't help but feel grateful for the fact that she could well afford better than this now. Her family had all been dead against her becoming a journalist because it wasn't like 'getting a proper trade' and even though she'd been with the Manchester Evening Chronicle for nearly five years now they still didn't acknowledge what she did as being a 'proper job'. And even though she'd moved into the city centre and got herself a flat in the Northern quarter, it still wasn't good enough for a family that didn't recognise anything beyond their own narrow sphere. Her sister had got three kids by three different fathers and was living in a grotty council house in Fallowfield but she'd made it as far as Sharon's family, especially her mother, was concerned. Sharon who had her career, her own flat, her own car and a sizeable disposable income that she often used to help her sister out, was considered some kind of failure. She had a job when the majority of her extended family didn't but she was still considered as some kind of failure. They thought she was trying to be 'above herself'. They thought she was turning her back on them when all she wanted was their approval and just some kind of acknowledgment that she'd done well.

So here she was sitting amongst those who her family would consider had made it. There was the man sitting in the corner who looked like he hadn't washed since Victoria was on the throne, happily chomping away into a plate of fish and chips that he'd mashed and mixed into a pulp with ketchup, mayonnaise, and vinegar. He was getting half of it down his already filthy shirt but he didn't seem to bother. Then there was the mother who was feeding the occasional chip to a toddler who was screaming in his pushchair desperate to get out and driven mad by the restraints he was under and the fact that he'd probably not been talked to properly or eaten a decent meal since the day he was born. His mother looked like Sharon's sister. Hair scraped back and in a ponytail. A face that said she hated life and the world and with eyes that looked upon her child as if she absolutely despised his very existence. She was pushing the pushchair back and forth with a nonchalant hand. Her family probably thought she'd made it too. That's if she had a family that is.

Then there was the family of the future standing at the order counter. Some young guy in his late teens with greasy hair and spots all over his face was holding hands with his girlfriend and complaining to the guy frying the chips that his mother had thrown him out after he told her his girlfriend was pregnant. They live in Bolton but he'd come over to Stockport to look for his Dad to see if he could put him up but he can't find him so he thinks he must've gone back inside. Sitting near him was a man who was dressed like Elvis and was shaking vinegar on top of his chip butty making deep brown stains all over the white bread. Sharon's sense of compassion kicked in and she couldn't help but feel sorry for all of them. Such shattered and broken lives under the one roof of a chippy with a sign that read 'toilets are on the bus station – thank you'.

'Sharon?'

Sharon looked up to see this beautiful young Indian girl looking down hopefully and yet nervously at her at the same time.

'Yes? That's me?'

'Oh good. I recognized your picture from your column in the paper but I still wanted to make sure'.

'You're Anita?' said Sharon.

'Yes. Anita Patel'.

Sharon stood up and shook hands. 'Thank you for coming to meet me but tell me, why did you want to meet here?'

'I always come in here for chips' said Anita. 'It's cheap'.

Sharon thought Anita was stunning. Her thick black hair was brushed off her face revealing large dark eyes. She was short, maybe a little over five feet tall, and was wearing a pair of tight blue jeans with a white t-shirt under a big baggy dark green v-necked sweater. Sharon thought Anita did casual much better than she herself did and her clothes ideally matched her feminine and gentle poise. And at least Anita looked like she'd ironed her clothes and there was no chipping of her bright pink nail polish that matched her bright pink lipstick. Sharon's nail polish was chipped and she wrapped her fingertips into her hands self-consciously. She usually threw on what she'd discarded the night before, usually in a heap at the side of her bed. But then she'd never given much thought to her appearance. It wasn't as important to her as the credit she gave herself for being bloody good at her job.

'How come you can eat chips and keep that wonderful figure?'

Anita blushed. 'I don't know. I'm lucky I suppose'.

'Anita, I want you to understand that you're under no pressure here'.

'That's good because … well I'm in my final few weeks of study and I've already booked my flight home to Mumbai. I don't want anything to go wrong. But the thought of some extra money to take back with me is tempting and was the reason why I decided to meet you in the end. I'm not from a rich family. When I go home with my degree and get a job in one of the new high tech companies that are springing up all over Mumbai I'll be able to earn some good money to support the family'.

'That's very good of you and I'll bet your family are very proud' said Sharon. 'Have you always worked at the Mayfair hotel since you've been here?'

'More or less' said Anita. 'I liked the job at first'.

'Why do you say at first?'

'Well I mean it was nice to work in that hotel environment' Anita explained. 'Then the shine started to come off when I realised just what kind of services I was supposed to offer'.

Sharon had been given the job by her boss of investigating the alleged prostitution ring run by Manchester gangster Bernie Connolly and that included several of the city's hotels along with some on the outskirts of the Greater Manchester area like the Mayfair. If they could crack what was going on then the Chronicle would indeed have managed a major scoop and Sharon knew it would enhance her journalistic reputation but the staff at the big city centre hotels weren't playing so she'd approached staff at the Mayfair, beginning with Anita.

'I have to be able to trust you, Sharon' Anita went on.

'You can trust me implicitly, Anita'.

'I mean, I still have a few weeks to go before I go home and I don't know what they'd do if they knew I'd talked to you'.

'Your name will not be mentioned in the paper, Anita, and I shall not pass it on to anybody else. You have my word on that. I only approached you that day when you were on duty behind the reception desk because I sensed there was a story you could tell me. And because my paper had received a tip-off'.

'A tip off?' asked Anita, suddenly panicked. 'It didn't mention me, did it?'

'No, no, I can assure you it didn't, Anita. Now please you've got to trust me, love. I would never drop you in it'.

Anita began breathing more evenly and then said 'Okay'.

'So tell me the basics first'

'Around half a dozen of the members of staff work as prostitutes in the hotel'.

'In addition to their normal duties?'

'Yes' said Anita. 'There are five girls and one boy who's from the Czech Republic and he's gorgeous. No wonder he makes so much extra cash. And he'll do men as well as women'.

'It pays to be versatile' said Sharon. 'And where do you come in?'

'I have to suggest to guests who I think may be up for it that the hotel offers other kinds of services' Anita explained. Then she shivered as if something was crawling all over her. 'A couple of times the guest has reported me to the manager but of course they're not going to do anything because I'm following orders'.

'And how much do you get for your troubles?'

'Nothing'.

'Nothing?'

'Not a penny piece. The ones who do it have to charge the guest one hundred pounds and the staff member has to give eighty of it up'.

'So they only make twenty quid each time?'

'Yes' said Anita. 'It's the night manager's job to make sure they don't run off with the full hundred'.

Sharon sat back in her plastic chair. 'Why do they do it?'

'Sharon, we are all foreign, a long way from home, we're all here to make money and learn better English but most importantly, none of us want to come up against a local gangster'.

'The local gangster being?'

'Bernie Connelly' Anita revealed. 'I don't know how much he makes and how much goes to Mr and Mrs Curzon but they somehow share the eighty pounds'.

'And how much are we talking about in total say, per week?'

'About fifteen hundred, two thousand pounds a week'.

'Have they asked you? I'm surprised if they haven't because you're beautiful'

'Yes but I refused' said Anita. 'They gave me a hard time for a while but then they got some other girls and left me alone after that'.

'Anita, was this going on the night when the body of James Clifton was found at the hotel?'

'Yes' Anita confirmed. She held her hand to her mouth. She felt sick when she thought of James Clifton. 'Two of the girls and the boy were both on jobs in the hotel that night'.

'But James Clifton wasn't involved?'

'No' said Anita. 'He wasn't staying at the hotel and I'd never heard of him before'.

'I'll need the names of those three who were working that night, Anita'.

'Yes, but look, you've got to make sure they don't know it's me who told you'.

'Anita, they won't find out. I promised you before and I meant it. Now, do you know anything about what happened to James Clifton last weekend?'

Anita's eyes welled up with tears. 'Oh Sharon, I've done a terrible thing but if the police find out I know they won't let me go home'.

FIREFLIES THIRTEEN

Paula Jones had never got used to sleeping alone. She'd had enough practice with her sales executive husband Phillip spending at least one night a week away from home for the last few years but she'd never really liked it. She wished she could get used to it. She wished she could be like all the other wives who drop their husbands off at Manchester airport who give them a kiss and a wave before driving off and relishing a night in front of the TV with the remote control and a box of chocolates. But the fact is she'd never been able to celebrate even in a small way any separation from her 'boys'. Her husband Rhodri and her son Piers were the centre of her world and always had been. Now Piers was about to fly the nest but the girl he was marrying couldn't have been better if Paula had chosen her herself. Clarissa came from a very good family in old money Cheshire and one day they would inherit a farm and an estate worth several million. And yet they were such lovely people. Sometimes Clarissa's mother even did her own cooking. She said it helped her to understand the lives of the people who work for her. Paula thought that was a fantastic meeting of the two very different realities and a terrific gesture of support for those less fortunate.

She did herself the usual breakfast of muesli and coffee before checking her phone to see if there were anymore messages. There was a new one from Rhodri who was in Helsinki where, due to the two hour time difference in their favour, the working day was already underway. He was due to fly back to Manchester that afternoon and Paula was going to be at the airport to pick him up from the Finnair flight. She'd be so pleased to have him back. She always was.

Then she re-read the one she'd had from her darling boy Piers at two o'clock that morning. He'd been out on his stag night and he knew that she was worried so he'd texted to reassure her that he was okay. They'd gone for a Thursday because they were planning other activities for the weekend culminating in a lunch party that Paula and Rhodri were throwing for their Piers and their family and friends on Sunday. It was going to be one hell of a weekend of partying and Piers was no doubt sleeping it off somewhere with one of his friends. He'd be back later for dinner with his parents, one of the last ones the three of them would share together by themselves before he got married. Paula felt that lump in her throat when she thought of it. Piers was their only child and both she and Rhodri were going to miss him so much.

She went out to her car and threw her briefcase on the passenger seat before reversing out of the drive and turning left down the lane to head for the main road a couple of miles away. The village where they lived was attached to the town of Wilmslow by the open field equivalent of a short umbilical cord. She liked it round here. It was full of people who didn't care about anything except their own self interests.

She drove past the pub which Paula would have to admit wasn't always welcoming to outsiders. She'd sometimes taken visiting friends in there and the landlady had made great store out of deliberately serving her regulars before people who'd never been in there before. But that was one of the drawbacks of living in a village. People could be rather more inward looking than even Paula would always appreciate.

There were half a dozen houses to the left of the lane as it climbed up the hill and out of the village. To the right were uninhibited and quite magnificent views across the Cheshire plains and even though she'd lived there now for thirteen years she still marveled at the view especially on a bright morning like this one.

She went down to second gear as the climb grew steeper and she pushed down harder on the accelerator. She knew the route like the back of her hand and almost didn't even have to think about it but as she neared the fork in the road where it branched off to the other side of the village whilst the other side carried on towards the main road, her eyes touched on the base of one of the overhanging trees and the sight that met her eyes made her gasp with horror. She stopped the car and got out to get a closer view. Then she screamed at the sight of the body of her son Piers, clearly dead, naked and having been sat upright against the tree trunk, covered in blood and with everything that made him a man missing.

Round his neck was a sign that said 'Have a Nice Day, Mum. X'

When a third person moves into a house where previously two have had the place to themselves for a while, a little adjusting of hitherto acceptable behavior needs to take place. Two nights ago Brendan the nanny moved in with Jeff and Toby and now Jeff was aware that he couldn't just walk from the bathroom to his bedroom naked anymore. Brendan seemed like a mature lad for his tender age of twenty-two but the last thing Jeff needed at the moment was to awaken a gay man's curiosity about him with the sight of his naked form. It was the same consideration he'd show if a young girl had moved in. So from now on he was going to make sure he wore his bathrobe whenever he was walking around without any clothes on.

Jeff and Toby had interviewed Brendan together and they'd all got along like a house on fire. Brendan was the oldest of five kids and he was used to looking after the young ones in his family which was one of the things that prompted him into making a career out of child care. He and Toby had bonded over the computer games console and Jeff could see it was good for a little boy to have a male nanny because Brendan would be able to do all the boy stuff that Jeff couldn't do when he wasn't there. He wasn't worried any longer that Toby didn't have enough female influence in his life. As Rebecca and also his brother Lewis had pointed out Toby had his Chinese grandma and aunts, his teacher at school Miss Jackson, and their next door neighbour Pam who Toby spent a fair amount of time with. He'd probably never stop worrying about Toby and whether or not he'd grow up right. He'd never stop worrying if he was doing right by him. It was part of the weight of being a single parent.

When Jeff had got home last night Brendan had done all the ironing and hung all his shirts and trousers neatly in his wardrobe. He hadn't expected that. And now as he walked downstairs and into the kitchen where Brendan presented him with a fry up of eggs, bacon, sausage, mushrooms, and baked beans, he hadn't expected that either. He hadn't really talked to Brendan about the definition of his role but he'd sort of thought that it would just revolve around Toby. He hadn't expected to be looked after himself too.

'Morning Brendan' said Jeff. 'This looks great. How are you finding everything?'

'Just fine, thanks, Jeff' Brendan answered with a smile. 'I made a pot of tea when I heard you upstairs because I know how you like it to have brewed for a bit before you drink it'.

'Well yes' said Jeff, a little shyly. 'Thank you. But you know, you don't have to go to all this trouble for breakfast, Brendan'.

'You need a good breakfast inside you if you're going to be running round catching criminals all day and I don't mind at all' said Brendan. 'All part of the service'.

'And thank you too for sorting my shirts and all' said Jeff. 'They've never been as tidy'.

'Jeff, I've got to have something to do when Toby is at school' said Brendan. 'That's when I do the washing, do the ironing, and generally keep things up to scratch in the house'.

'Well then, thank you. That's very kind'.

'Don't mention it' said Brendan who had the feeling he was going to rather like working here. Toby was a grand little lad and Jeff was one of the nicest straight men he'd ever met.

Handsome too but Brendan didn't think anything more than that. He was here to do a job and anyway, Jeff may be gay friendly but that's as far as it went.

Jeff looked at Toby who was tucking eagerly into scrambled eggs on toast. 'Shall we keep Brendan, Toby?'

'Yeah he's cool' said Toby. 'And he cooks better than you, Daddy'.

'Well that's it then, Brendan' said Jeff. 'The deal is well and truly done'.

'I'm glad' said Brendan who felt lucky that this was his first full-time post. Some of his friends had experienced nightmares in their first jobs. 'This is a dream job believe me. Some of them on my course haven't been so lucky and some haven't been able to get anything'.

'Widowers with kids to look after are more common than society thinks' said Jeff. 'There must be more families like ours to look after out there?'

'Well there's also of course the fact that there's still a stigma attached to men looking after kids in the eyes of some'.

'Well this house is a stigma free zone, Brendan' said Jeff after he'd swallowed a piece of bacon. 'And by the way, how did you know I like my bacon this way?'

Brendan blushed. 'I asked your brother Lewis'.

Jeff smiled. 'I see. And what else has he told you about my habits? No, on second thoughts don't answer that'.

'You and him are pretty close, right?'

'Yeah, we are' said Jeff. 'Uncle Lewis is a star in our world, isn't he, Toby?'

'Yes' said Toby. 'And don't forget Uncle Seamus, Daddy'.

'How could I forget Uncle Seamus? Now, if you've finished your scrambled eggs, big boy then go up and brush your teeth and I'll take you to school'.

'Okay Daddy' said Toby who then ran off in the direction of the stairs in his usual whirlwind little boy way. Jeff watched him running and felt that surge of emotion that every parent feels when they somehow want to stop their child from growing up and having to deal with this increasingly horrible world. Poor Toby had already had to deal with the loss of his mother and Jeff was determined to protect him as much as he could for as long as he could from any further pain or hurt.

'Toby seems like a well adjusted kid considering what he's been through' said Brendan.

'He's coped remarkably well, Brendan' said Jeff. 'But that doesn't stop me from worrying about what's going on under the surface and what the long term effects of losing his Mum so young might be'.

'How long do you think she'll be staying, love?'

'Are you saying she's outstayed her welcome, Gran?' asked Andrea, anxiously. She hoped her Gran wasn't going off her friend. 'I mean, Tina is paying her way after all'.

'No, I'm not saying that at all, Andrea' said her Gran. 'And I appreciate that she's paying her way. I just wondered that was all'.

It had been twelve years since Andrea had moved in with her Grandma. She was only eleven at the time but life at 'home' would've become intolerable for her.

She'd known from an early age that her parents weren't happy. She'd often felt like she was the link that kept them together and she'd quickly got to know what her mother meant when she described her father as an adulterous liar. It meant all the times she shut herself away in her room with her fingers in her ears whilst her parents slugged it out with each other downstairs. They'd had a business together in Blackpool, a hotel with fifteen bedrooms near the Central pier and all the attractions of the Golden mile. Sometimes it got a little noisy, especially at weekends, but her mother used to just take everything in her stride and provide a motherly influence on young lads and lasses who thought they could hold their drink when really they couldn't hold a toilet seat by the time they got back from partying.

It was during one of those nights when her mother had been trying to diffuse any violent clashes with her husband by going out with her friends that Andrea caught her father kissing another woman. She hadn't been a guest at the hotel. Andrea found out later that they'd met at an exhibition in Manchester of hotel businesses and ways to improve your hotel property for the modern age, but her eyes had been frozen at the sight of this bitch being so intimate with her father. When the woman saw her she used her foot to slam the door shut but seconds later it opened again and her father came running after her. But he didn't catch up with her and when she sneaked back to the private flat in the hotel that she shared with her parents, Andrea heard the woman say to her father that 'she would have to know sometime' and 'you'll have to tell her that Daddy won't be around for much longer and that it'll be better for all concerned if they make a clean break and wait until she's older so she can decide if she wants any contact'. Andrea was heartbroken. This woman who stared at her with such hatred was planning to take her Daddy away from her and her Mummy. She was only eleven years old and yet she understood perfectly well what was happening. 'She's been no good to you for years. With me by your side we could really go somewhere. You know what it's like between us. A fire like this doesn't come along more than once in life and we've got to grab it with everything we've got. And if that means letting go of what's gone before then we have

to do that or else life won't forgive us. It just won't. Now don't be weak, Brian. Be strong'.

Andrea's mother had overheard that particular part of her husband's lovers entreaty and it

had made her sick. She'd tried her best to be a good wife and she couldn't stand to hear her

husband being tempted away so blatantly. It had taken away all that had been left of her pride

and her self-belief.

The next morning Andrea found her mother dead in bed. She'd taken an overdose. The

empty bottle of paracetemol was lying beside her open hand. Her eyes were open there was a

trail of dried up vomit coming out of the corner of her mouth. It somehow didn't occur to

Andrea to call her father because she had no idea where he was. But with a shaking hand she

was able to call an ambulance and call her grandma who came over immediately to be with

her as well as dealing with her own grief over the loss of her daughter in such tragic

circumstances. She'd already lost her beloved husband Frank several years before and now

she'd lost her dear daughter too. But she had to be there for her granddaughter. Poor Andrea

was in a terrible state and she should never have had to find her mother like that.

Brian Curzon hadn't expected a slap across the face from his mother-in-law Marjorie

when he came home later that morning. He hadn't expected to find that his wife had taken the

exit door from life either.

'You've got to take this as an opportunity, Brian' Helen reasoned. 'We've been lovers for

so long and we've been waiting for the right chance for you to make that break and here it is.

She was weak, Brian, weak and feeble. You're better off without her and you know it'.

Andrea came up behind them and smashed a vase across Helen's back. Helen swung

round 'You horrible little bitch! You've drawn blood!' She raised her hand to slap her but

Andrea, who was almost as tall as Helen, stopped her arm in mid air and gripped it like a python grips its prey.

'If you so much as touch me I'll tell the world that Daddy has been touching me in a bad way for years' Andrea threatened.

Helen turned to Brian who was stood motionless and panic stricken 'Brian?'

'It isn't true, I swear, she's just lost her mother and she's firing out because she's in shock'.

Helen turned back to Andrea. 'So you're a liar too'.

'Can you afford to take that risk?'

'You're pure evil'.

'No, I'm looking at pure evil' said Andrea. 'And one day I'll get you back for killing my mother'.

'She killed herself because she was weak and pathetic!'

'Shut your stupid mouth!'

'Oh what's the matter? Don't like hearing the truth? Well I'm going to be the proper supportive wife to your father that he's always needed. You can do what you like'.

Later that evening Andrea went home with her Grandma and that's where she stayed. Brian Curzon sold the Blackpool hotel he'd co-owned with his wife and invested the money in the Mayfair in Stockport which Helen already owned. Helen and Brian were married a month later.

Andrea hugged her Gran. 'You've been so good to me, Gran. I'm just trying to help a friend like you helped me'.

'And I'm proud of you for doing that, love'.

'It's depends what the police say' said Andrea. 'If they drop the charges then I think Tina will go home fairly soon. If they don't drop the charges and carry on with them then … well I really don't know what will happen but Tina won't have any choice about where she lives then'.

FIREFLIES FOURTEEN

It was never an easy job for a police officer to visit the parents of someone who'd been murdered. In the case of Rhodri and Paula Jones it was going to be especially difficult because of the circumstances in which Paula Jones had found the body of her son. It had sent her into a not surprisingly hysterical state and she'd had to be sedated but now, several hours later and with her husband Rhodri having returned from his business trip to Helsinki, she said she wanted to talk to the police.

'Mrs. Jones?' said Jeff, gently. 'We'd first of all like to say how sorry we are for your loss'.

'Thank you, detective' she replied in a meak voice. She was sitting on the sofa holding hands with Rhodri. They looked so lost like two little kids in search of their missing parents. They'd also both been crying. They seemed to be overwhelmed by the tragedy they were facing. 'Have you arrested Tina Webb?'

'Mrs. Jones, Tina Webb has an alibi for last night'.

'Well she's lying!'

'Mrs. Jones, there's also other evidence suggesting that Tina Webb wasn't responsible for your son's murder' Jeff explained. He watched Paula Jones look up to the heavens with a look of disbelieving disgust and then shake her head. 'You'll have to trust us'.

'What kind of evidence?' asked Rhodi Jones through gritted teeth.

When the body of Piers Jones was taken by the pathologist June Hawkins to her lab she found, despite the state he was in, DNA to suggest that Piers had experienced sexual intercourse before he died. And the DNA wasn't that of Tina Webb and nor did it match anything they had on the database.

'We'll talk about that later, Mr. Jones' said Jeff who didn't think they'd want to hear about their son's rampant sexual activity on the night of his murder. 'We need to ask you a little about Piers. How was he getting on with his fiancée Clarissa?'

'They were getting on fine' said Paula, her eyes welling up with tears again. 'They were absolutely made for each other. Everybody said that. They were blissfully happy and couldn't wait to spend the rest of their lives together'.

Rebecca watched Rhodri as his wife spoke. From the look on his face he didn't exactly concur with the picture his wife was painting of their son and his fiancée.

'Would you agree with that, Mr. Jones?' Rebecca asked.

Rhodri paused and his wife questioned. 'Rhodri?'

Rhodri squeezed his wife's hand. 'My darling there are some things you don't know'.

'What things?' Paula demanded almost hysterically. 'What have you been keeping from me?'

'I only kept it from you because I didn't want you to worry'.

'What? Damn you, tell me!'

'Piers was having an affair with another girl and he was having serious second thoughts about marrying Clarissa'.

Paula placed her hand on her chest. 'It's not true'.

'It is true, Paula' said Rhodri who then pulled his wife close and held her tight.

'Well did Clarissa find out?'

'I believe she did and that Piers had managed to assure her that it had all been a big mistake and he'd ended the affair'.

'And had he?'

'No' said Rhodri. 'He lied to her because the girl he was having an affair with told him she was pregnant with his child'.

Paula screamed. 'The stupid, the stupid little fool!'

As Jeff and Rebecca walked up the stairs to the first floor flat just off Palatine road in Chorlton of Annette Bryson, they were clearly going to be walking into a situation with the noise that was coming from behind her door.

'Well if you hadn't been the rotten little slag who'd open her legs for any passing fiver then you wouldn't be in this mess!'

'Mum, how could you? How could you say that to me when I'm in this state?'

'What on earth is Pastor Edwards going to say? You've brought shame on the whole congregation by getting pregnant out of wedlock! Of course your father wanted me to go easy on you but then he's always been soft where Daddy's little girl is concerned. It's always been me who's had to instill the discipline in our children'.

'Yes, Mum, and we've all got the scars to prove it and I don't mean just on the inside'.

'It was for your own good'.

'Oh spare me! You ruled us all with fear because you weren't capable of showing love! You're just another pathetic excuse for a human being who hides her weakness behind religious intolerance. Here I am, your daughter, your pregnant daughter who's just lost the father of her unborn child to some sick individual and you're incapable of reaching out to me with anything that might be comfort or support. What does that say about you, Mum? Well I tell you what it says. It says that you didn't deserve to have children'.

'If you hadn't rejected the word of the good Lord you wouldn't be in this immoral mess!'

'You're a nasty, vicious, cruel woman and I'm ashamed, yes ashamed to call you my mother'.

'You dare to speak to me like that. The devil has truly taken hold of your soul'.

'Just get out Mum and never, ever come anywhere near me ever again'.

Jeff was about to knock on the door when it burst open and a tall black woman in her late fifties and looking eminently respectable in her hat and long tailored coat came darting out.

'Who are you?' she demanded.

'The police' said Jeff. 'We're here to speak to … '

' … if you want to speak to that slut who used to be my daughter then feel free. I wash my hands of her'.

And with that she was gone. Jeff and Rebecca ventured inside and found Annette in a heap in the middle of the living room floor crying her heart out. Rebecca managed to get her up and onto the sofa where she sat next to her and put her arm round her shoulder. Jeff went into the kitchen and brought her a glass of water.

'Thank you' said Annette who Jeff thought was a really pretty girl with big dark eyes and hair down to her shoulder blades. She was shaking.

'Have you got someone who can come and sit with you, Annette?' asked Rebecca.

'Yes, my sister Rochelle' said Annette. 'She's been in London with work and she's on her way back up on the train now'.

'Who told you about Piers?' asked Jeff.

'His father rang me' Annette answered. 'He thought I had a right to know. He's such a kind man. He's promised to look after me when … when the baby comes'.

'How far gone are you?' asked Rebecca.

'Five months'.

'And how long had you been seeing Piers?'

'Just over a year' said Annette in a slightly whimpering voice. 'I met him on a night out with friends, you know, the usual kind of thing. He came back with me that night and the next morning he asked to see me again and it went from there. We fell in love and he was very conflicted because of Clarissa. I knew they were engaged but I also knew he wasn't happy with her and though that's what you'd expect me to say it was true. He wasn't happy with her but he couldn't … he just couldn't manage to pull himself away'.

'He was on his stag night, Annette' said Jeff.

'Yes, yes, I know! I know it sounds like I'm being some stupid delusional little girl who pinned all her hopes on a man who just wanted to have his cake and eat it. I've had my nose rubbed in all that more than once, detective'.

Rebecca's heart was going out to Annette but it also made her think of what she had going on with Jonathan Freeman. Although she was beginning to find him somewhat arrogant and opinionated they'd slept together another couple of times because he was wonderful in bed and she didn't want to cut off her nose to spite her face by denying herself the many carnal pleasures he gave her. But he did seem to have a negativity towards Ollie Wright for some reason but which nevertheless made her agree with Jeff Barton that Ollie would never have spread rumours about Jeff and herself. So had Jonathan been making it all up?

'Your mother seemed pretty angry when she left' said Rebecca who still had her arm round Annette who was still shaking.

'Oh she'd have me burned at the stake if she had her way' said Annette, bitterly. 'Five kids and not one of them ever goes to see her. But instead of wondering why that might be she turns it back on us and somehow makes it all our fault for not following her ways. She's got a heart of stone that one. She was almost sadistic when we were kids. But like child batterers always say she did it for our own good. No hugs, no cuddles, no smiles ever on her face, just this stern, determined look as if she was about to lead the army into battle. God only knows what my Dad ever saw in her. No joy on birthdays with presents or cakes. We had to devote the day as thanksgiving to the good Lord for giving us life and we were just slaves to her interpretation of religious dogma at Christmas too. It's going to be so different for my child. They'll know they're loved and needed and cared for. Their life will be full of fun and laughter. They won't know what fear is and I'm not going to allow my mother anywhere near them'.

'It'll be her grandchild'.

'I'm her daughter but that didn't stop her beating me to within an inch of my life when she thought I was possessed by the devil or some other such nonsense that filled her nasty head'.

'Annette, you know we have to ask you' said Jeff.

'What was I doing last night? I understand. Well yes, Piers was here and we made love' She wiped the tears from her cheeks with her hands. 'He was afraid he might hurt the baby, you know, and I had to reassure him it was all okay and he didn't need to worry. Then afterwards he started to cry. He said he felt like his life was out of his control and he was hurtling towards something he just didn't want. He didn't want to marry Clarissa. He wanted me and our baby but he was under pressure from his mother and from Clarissa herself'.

'We'll have to take a DNA sample, Rebecca' said Jeff who was glad to have discovered who Piers Jones had slept with the night he died. At least that wasn't going to be another gaping hole in the investigation.

'I thought you would and yes, of course that's fine'.

'What happened next, Annette?'

'I made him a coffee and we talked some more' said Annette. 'I was surprised at how well he was. I could tell he'd had a drink but he wasn't pissed. Then he headed off to some nightclub he knew where his mates would be waiting for him'.

'And what time was that?'

'About three' said Annette, holding back more tears when she thought of the last time she'd seen Piers. 'He'd been with me since about one. Oh God what am I going to do?'

Annette started sobbing again and Rebecca held her close and tight. 'Now come on, Annette, sweetheart. I know it must seem like the bottom has fallen out of your world but that baby growing inside you is going to need the wonderful mother who I know you'll be. Kind, loving, everything your own mother isn't. You've got to find it in you to be strong, Annette. You've got to find it in you somehow even though I know how hard it must be'.

'My baby will never know their father'.

'They will because you'll keep his memory alive and you'll tell your child all about his father'.

They all heard the sound of something coming through the letterbox and Jeff went to pick it up. It was a padded brown envelope with Annette's name hand written on it.

'Were you expecting anything, Annette?' asked Jeff.

'No? What is it?'

'I don't know but you don't have to open it now' said Jeff. He turned it over and on the back was written 'Something to remember him by and this is all you'll get'.

'That's a strange thing to have written, don't you think?' said Annette.

'It does seem odd' said Jeff. 'Do you want me to open it?'

'No, it's okay' said Annette. She took the envelope from him and tore it open. Then she screamed before dropping it and throwing up.

Jeff picked up the envelope. Blood came flowing out of it and inside were a man's genitals.

Jeff and Rebecca called a doctor and arranged for a female uniformed officer to come and stay with Annette until the doctor had been and her sister Rochelle had arrived from London.

'Poor Annette' said Rebecca in the car on the way back to the station. 'She was hanging on to such slim hope it seems to me and yet she was so in love with the man'.

'None as blind as those who won't see, eh?' said Jeff.

'Well she isn't the first woman in her position' said Rebecca. 'But the story doesn't usually end with the man's private parts being delivered to her like that. What kind of a sick, twisted mind are we looking at here?'

'One that I'm even more determined to get now' said Jeff. 'At least we know who Piers Jones had sex with before somebody got to him and his bollocks'.

'We're ruling out Annette as a suspect then I presume?'

'Well do you think we should rule her in?'

'No' said Rebecca. 'She's even less capable than Tina Webb. But who the fuck is responsible and where does the death of Piers Jones leave us in terms of finding out?'

.

FIREFLIES FIFTEEN

When Jeff and Rebecca got back to the station the sergeant on reception called Jeff over and told him that someone was waiting in the interview room for him by the name of Seamus Enright.

'Seamus?' said Jeff as he entered the interview room to the side of the reception desk where his brother Lewis' partner was sitting there in his airline pilot's uniform. 'What are you doing here, mate? Is it our Lewis?'

'Oh no, Jeff' said Seamus who stood up. He'd come straight from work. 'Sorry if I worried you. It's not about Lewis, he's fine'.

'Phew!' said Jeff as he gave Seamus a bear hug. 'So what can I do for you?'

'Well' said Seamus as he sat down again. 'I don't know if this is something or nothing'.

'But?'

'Well you see last night I was on a stopover in Copenhagen' Seamus explained. 'I went out to dinner with the rest of the team and one of the cabin crew was a new girl called Melanie Cartwright. As soon as I'd set eyes on her earlier in the day I knew she reminded me of someone. I mentioned it to her over dinner and she seemed very uncomfortable about it, almost defensive which I thought was a little unusual. Anyway, one bottle of wine led to another, then we all went back to the hotel and went into the bar for nightcaps. At the end of the evening it was only me and Melanie left and she literally burst into tears on my shoulder. She said she'd done something she shouldn't have and she was scared she was going to get sacked because she was still on her initial three months trial. And it was whilst we were talking that I remembered who she reminded me of'.

'Who?'

'Sophie Cooper' said Seamus. 'Jeff, Melanie is the spitting image of Sophie Cooper and when I said that she looked absolutely horrified and said goodnight before running up to her room. Then today we did the flight back to Manchester this morning and then a quick return to Edinburgh and back but for all three flights she avoided me and ran like the bloody clappers when our duty finished. I spoke to the in-charge cabin crew member and he said that he thought there was something odd about her. He said she was jumpy all the time and seemed frightened of her own shadow'.

'So what are you telling me?' asked Jeff.

'Well I did a little digging with our crew roster department' Seamus went on. 'The night of the murder of James Clifton, Sophie Cooper's fiancé, Sophie was the only Manchester based crew member working with a team from our base at Leeds. You see, we mainly do scheduled flights to business destinations at Manchester as you know but the night Tenerife on a Saturday is something we've picked up for the summer season to get more revenue out of working the fleet harder. But the cabin crew training hasn't caught up so at the moment we crew it mainly from our Leeds base with one of our Manchester crew there to make up the numbers. The pilots were also both from the Leeds base. Now if none of them knew Sophie because they'd never worked with her before because they were from a different base, then Melanie could've easily passed for Sophie because we don't stand there studying each other's ID badges. Now I know Sophie and I know what a bully she can be with some of the younger new girls. Can you see where I'm going with this?'

'So you're saying that this Melanie could've gone to work in place of Sophie Cooper that night because Sophie Cooper put pressure on her and none of the rest of the crew would've been any the wiser because they weren't from the Manchester base?'

'Yes, Jeff, that's exactly what I'm saying'.

'But how? I mean, I thought you all swiped into your report centre with your ID badge and your own personal pin code? And swiped out again when you're done?'

'We do' Seamus confirmed. 'But what if Sophie had given Melanie her ID badge so that she could go to work for Sophie that night? What if they'd both gone into work, both in uniform, and then swapped ID badges before the Leeds crew arrived? The records will show that Melanie Cartwright left the crew room probably only minutes later whilst Sophie Cooper didn't leave until the end of her duty the next morning. But really it was the other way round. It is possible, Jeff'.

'You're making some big leaps here, Seamus' said Jeff who nevertheless was letting his imagination turn onto the scenario Seamus had worked out.

'Yes, I might be' said Seamus. 'But then again, I might not be'.

It wasn't difficult to find the answers they needed. Jeff sent Ollie Wright out to Manchester airport to look at the access system into the crew reporting centre where both Sophie Cooper and Melanie Cartwright signed in to work. As was usually the case these days with airports the presence of CCTV everywhere made the job of the police easier and once Ollie had got through all the flirting that Dean, the tall, fat and rather camp cabin crew manager was inflicting on him, he managed to get to the footage that he needed. He didn't mind Dean flirting with him. He found it quite funny and though Dean wasn't at all his type he always found it flattering when someone clearly had the eye for him. Ollie and his partner Josh had an arrangement whereby they allowed each other sexual adventures with third parties as long as they kept it to themselves and didn't exchange telephone numbers with whoever they got off with. They loved each other dearly and had a good sex life. But their cocks required a little more freedom and variety from time to time. It was an arrangement that some wouldn't understand but they were the ones who couldn't see that having sex with someone else didn't mean you loved your partner any less. Emotional fidelity was important to Ollie and Josh. Physical fidelity wasn't something they attached any importance to so long as they did it discreetly and didn't rub each other's nose in it.

What Ollie saw on the tape turned out to be just as Seamus Enright had imagined. Both Sophie Cooper and Melanie Cartwright swiped their ID's and entered the crew reporting centre at 8.27 on that Saturday night, both in full uniform. Nine minutes later at 8.36 'Melanie Cartwright' swiped out again. Except that on the tape it was clearly Sophie Cooper who was leaving at 8.36 with a nervous look around her as she went. She wasn't seen again and the woman known as Melanie Cartwright didn't leave until the next morning although according to the security swipe she was Sophie Cooper.

When Sharon Bellfield first came out of university her father insisted she take any job she could find because he'd 'given her more than her fair share already'. So she managed to secure a job in the typing pool of one of the last remaining textile firms just outside Bolton. The place was full of two-legged relics. Even the younger members of staff acted like they'd already been downtrodden by the sharp realities of life. They didn't have a rank structure amongst the typists but one of the girls who called herself a 'senior' was called Anne. Sharon absolutely detested her. She was never seen without a packet of crisps in her hand which was nothing in itself but which irritated the shit out of Sharon because it meant that wherever Anne was there was this crunching sound of crisps being devoured in her stupid mouth. She never seemed to eat anything else either. She never brought any sandwiches in or a bowl of salad or pasta. But she took it upon herself to come down hard on anyone who said they enjoyed a drink because of the example of some distant uncle in Darlington or some other such place who was a drunk. Sharon argued with her that just because someone likes a drink it doesn't make them a drunk, violent or otherwise. But this was how it is with people like Anne. They're such dull people leading such dull, pointless lives because they haven't got the guts to go out and get a good one that they come down hard on people like Sharon who like to go out and enjoy themselves. She always wore the most disgustingly old-fashioned clothes and she could moan and complain for England but the thing that really bugged Sharon about Anne was that despite having the disposition of a wet weekend in Scarborough she always signed her departmental notes 'Annie' and she always turned the dot on the i into a flower.

'Welcome to the Mayfair hotel, Stockport, how can I help you?'

'Yes, hello' said Sharon. She was impressed that Anita greeted her at the reception desk playing the game well and showing no signs that she was pretending she'd never met Sharon before. 'I have a reservation for this evening'.

'Okay, and the name is, please?'

'It's Annie Flower' said Sharon who always used Annie Flower's name when she needed a disguise. She wondered for a moment what the daft cow was doing now. Probably still eating crisps all day in some office environment where she pretended to be a senior. 'Miss Annie Flower'.

After her previous meetings with Anita Patel, Sharon had decided to check in to the Mayfair hotel to find out for herself any evidence suggesting it was one part of a wider prostitution ring involving staff in hotels across Greater Manchester. But this was only to be part of the investigation. She was keeping the most shocking revelation Anita had told her, about what she knew of what happened the night three years ago when Kim Barnes was murdered on her wedding night in the Manchester Hilton, to provide the kind of twist in a story that would make her journalistic career. But she needed to be careful. Anita could be in grave danger once her information is out but Sharon wasn't sure if she could keep her powder dry until Anita was safely back with her family in India.

Sharon was then approached by Anita's Czech male colleague Tomas who worked as a concierge who offered to carry her case to her room. And Anita had been right. Tomas was gorgeous. Tall and burly with big shoulders, neatly kept short blond hair and the most appealing green eyes. A quick look downstairs and Sharon didn't think she'd be disappointed with his packet either. He looked like a big boy and although she wasn't a size Queen she didn't like small dicks.

'So do you always escort guests to their rooms, Tomas?' Sharon asked after they'd come out of the lift at the second floor and were walking down the corridor.

'Sometimes' Tomas replied in his typically Eastern European accented English. 'We need to special care of customers because we had some troubles here last week. Police have been here asking all kinds of questions'.

'Because of the murder of James Clifton?'

'Yes' Tomas confirmed. 'But I did not tell you that. My boss doesn't like us to talk about it with guests'.

'Oh don't worry' said Sharon. 'Your secrets are safe with me, young man'.

Tomas smiled cheekily. 'I have no secrets'.

'I'm sure'.

They got to room 227 and Tomas opened the door and let Sharon go in. She was pleasantly surprised by the modern tasteful décor. She'd been expecting something rather different and old-fashioned.

'This is one of our newly refurbished rooms' said Tomas. 'Everything is touch button for curtains, lights and so on. And of course there is free Wifi in the room'.

'And what about room service?'

'Yes' said Tomas who by now had let the door close. He lifted up a book from the occasional table by the window and opened it out for her on the room service page. 'Here it is. Or we have restaurant downstairs'.

'How old are you, Tomas?'

'How old am I? Well I'm twenty-three but why do you ask such question?'

'You're here to earn money and improve your English?'

'Yes? But again I don't know why you ask?'

Sharon took off her coat and perched on the end of the bed. She outstretched her arms and placed her hands slightly behind her. Then she looked up at him. 'I was wondering if there was any special room service that you provide? I'm sure you know what I'm talking about' She watched Tomas's face lighten as the penny dropped. She slipped her foot out of her shoe and ran it up the inside of his lower leg. 'You're so handsome in that uniform by the way. I'm sure people have told you that before'

Tomas smiled. 'Would you like to see me out of it?'

'I would like that, yes' Sharon answered. She was almost whimpering like some daft teenager at the anticipation of seeing Tomas naked. He was ten years her junior and she really should remain professional but he was so bloody fit and a girl has needs. And besides she was a tabloid hack who'd stop at nothing to get to the heart of the real story. Nobody would expect her to act responsibly and just ask Tomas the questions she needed answers to. James Bond always fucked first and asked questions later. She was carrying on a fine old British tradition. The fact that she was a journalist and James Bond was a fictional secret agent was a mere detail. She knew what she meant and she'd be able to justify her actions to anybody.

Tomas stepped up close to her and stood coyly with his hands together behind his back. He leaned down and spoke softly. 'One hundred pounds cash for oral stimulation and the fuck of your life. When I'm hard I'm nine inches and I'm a very talented boy'.

'Fuck's sake' said Sharon, feeling giddy at the thought. 'Let me get my purse'.

'Oh and I'm in complete control'.

'I wouldn't have it any other way'.

Now Sharon had been around the block a few times but this would be recorded in her memoirs as a high point. Apart from the wonderful licking out he gave her, Tomas took her in the usual way of straight couples the world over but then he also took her from behind dog style, he took her over the back of the chair at the desk in the room, he took her up against the wall and when she was down on him she felt his fingers wave their way through her hair. She discovered that he was a master at holding off his orgasm, despite the obvious pleasures that were being unleashed, not least the orgasms Sharon was experiencing. And when he did let himself go he exploded inside her like a bomb shaking the very foundations of a building. It took her all her time not to scream the place down with joy.

'You weren't joking when you said you were a talented boy' said Sharon, breathlessly. She was lying on her back with Tomas beside her. She looked down and could see that he was still semi-hard. 'I suppose you go to the gym and all of that?'

'Yes, of course, every day. And you?'

'No' said Sharon. 'That's why I'm more out of breath than you are'.

Tomas leaned over and cupped her breast with his hand. He raised his thumb and used it to play with her nipple. 'I have to go soon. Anything else you want?'

'Information'.

'What?' asked Tomas, his face etched in confusion.

'I need information on the way this hotel is run, Tomas, with particular regard to the kind of room service I've just received. I'm not the police so don't worry about that. But I am in a position to pay you very handsomely, a lot more than a hundred quid, and your anonymity will be protected at all times. I can promise you that. So what do you say?'

'You have tricked me?' he asked looking almost angry.

'No, Tomas, I haven't tricked you' Sharon assured. 'I'm a journalist and I'm on your side'.

'I don't want my name in newspaper!'

'You won't get your name in the newspaper. You have to trust me, Tomas. Believe me it will be worth it to you financially and nobody will ever know that we talked except you and me'.

Tomas looked suspiciously at the door and then all around the room as if it might be bugged or something.

'Tomas, it's just you and me here' said Sharon. 'You're not in any trouble. Now do you like what you're doing here?'

'You don't like what I did to you?'

'Tomas, I loved what you did to me, any woman would. I'm asking if you wouldn't rather keep it all for your girlfriend?'

'I don't have girlfriend' Tomas declared. 'I don't mind having sex with lots of different people. I'm young and its fun for me'.

'But Tomas, wouldn't you rather keep all the money you make for yourself? What my newspaper can pay you would enable you to set yourself up, maybe in London, as a professional escort keeping every penny for yourself'.

Tomas still looked sceptical. He sat up and raised his knees before folding his hands in front of them. They were sitting there still naked, still winding down after their session. But Sharon had to get him on side if she was going to get to the heart of the story she was after.

'How much money?' Tomas asked.

'Four, maybe five figures?' Sharon suggested encouragingly. She had to get the balance right. If she was too pushy he'd run. 'Then you could say goodbye to all this and put those wonderful talents of yours into being your own boss. This is about you, Tomas, and the future you could have'.

FIREFLIES SIXTEEN

Jeff and Rebecca were driving to the Knutsford home of Manchester gangster Bernie Connelly and were intending to get there just as the team Jeff had ordered to serve a warrant on Connelly to search his house would be there and ready to start work.

'Do you think there is such a thing as an honest rich person?' said Rebecca as she looked at all the large houses that stank of money as they passed by them.

'Well I assume that all rich people employ accountants to find ways of getting them out of paying their fair share of tax so perhaps the answer to your question is no'.

Rebecca smiled. 'Yes, that's just what I was thinking. Jeff, you and Andy Kirkpatrick were really close, weren't you'.

'He was my best friend' said Jeff. 'We joined the force on the same day, went to college together, I was best man at his wedding. But I am aware of not letting the personal drive the professional'.

'I don't doubt that for a moment, Jeff' said Rebecca. 'How's Brendan the au pair settling in by the way?'

Jeff laughed. 'He's not an au pair, Becky'.

'That's what you'd call him if he was a girl'.

'Well okay, I guess you're right' said Jeff. 'He's actually settling in very nicely to tell you the truth. The house is clean and tidy for the first time in ages, he irons all my shirts and laundry and hangs everything up so I just have to reach out and put it on. And most importantly he gets on great with Toby. So all in all, it was a bloody good move to hire him'.

'He might develop a crush on you' she teased.

'Get out of it, Becky'.

'I'm sure it wouldn't be the first time a gay man had a crush on you, Jeff. Just like any young girl would. Being the caring, sharing, hands on modern Dad to Toby is a very alluring situation'.

'Yes, well Brendan it seems only has a crush on the Australian actor Hugh Jackman and as I look absolutely nothing like him I think I'm safe from even his fantasies'.

'Ah but you always end up with someone who looks nothing like what you think your ideal paramour looks like'.

'Yes, well I'm not going to go any further with this, DS Stockton' said Jeff. 'We'll be at Connelly's house soon'.

The raid they were about to perform on Connelly's house was part of a simultaneous operation that also included bringing Sophie Cooper, Clarissa Dalton-Wood, Melanie Cartwright, and Andrea Kay in for questioning. Ollie Wright had discovered that Sophie Cooper and Clarissa Dalton-Wood had been firm friends since they both started at Grange Park boarding school in Somerset when they were eleven years old and were in trouble throughout their time there. But in their last year there they were both expelled for sneaking out at night and getting drunk in the local pubs in the area. They had plenty of cash and were able to dress themselves up to look older than they were. But when they were expelled both sets of parents decided they wouldn't tolerate their behaviour any longer and they were both brought back home to the northwest where they went to Willowbrook comprehensive in Middleton, north Manchester. They settled in pretty quickly in terms of exercising more bad behaviour. They were both suspended, twice, for bullying two other students, namely

Melanie Cartwright and Andrea Kay but after that Andrea Kay became as thick as thieves with both Sophie and Clarissa. And when Ollie delved further he discovered that Andrea Kay's grandmother had for many years taken a sleeping pill every night that knocked her out for a good six or seven hours. And she's always in bed by eleven which would suggest that Andrea Kay was lying when she told Jeff and Rebecca that her grandmother always waited up for Andrea whenever she went out.

They were almost at Connelly's house when Jeff's mobile rung. He pressed the button on the dashboard so that he could answer it on speaker. It was Ollie Wright.

'Yes, Ollie?'

'Sir, Malcolm Barnes has been found dead at his house. The pathologist June Hawkins is there at the scene and she says it's the same as with James Clifton and Piers Jones. He's been castrated and probably drugged with rohipnol. She says the scene is pretty horrific'.

Tina Webb had thought it unusual that her friend Andrea Kay kept her bedroom door locked at all times whether she was at home or not. Not even Andrea's grandmother was allowed into her granddaughter's inner sanctum and Tina had tried not to think about it given that Andrea had been so good to her and she didn't want to risk feeling ungrateful by asking her what could turn out to be very personal questions. She was still staying with Andrea at Andrea's grandmother's house, in her own bedroom without a lock on it, because she couldn't stomach going home and being on her own whilst the police were still considering her to be under caution. But time was rolling on. They couldn't keep her in this kind of limbo land forever. She couldn't sleep. She was starting to drink far too much which was quite a thing for her. She'd always enjoyed a tipple or two but she was now self-medicating with alcohol and that wasn't good when she was also taking prescription tranquilisers.

Surely they must all know that she was innocent of this horrendous crime she'd been accused of? Somebody must've planted those knives covered in James Clifton's blood in her flat but why wouldn't anybody believe her except Andrea? She was the only one who'd stood by her throughout this nightmare.

But when she saw that Andrea's bedroom door wasn't locked for the first time since she'd been staying there curiosity got the better of her. Andrea's grandmother was out shopping and she could hear Andrea was in the shower. So she went in.

At first it looked like any other bedroom. There was a single bed in there but with a very little girl style of duvet cover featuring dolls or some other such girlee shit. It was all in pink and light blue. It wasn't to Tina's taste at all but she did know that Andrea was still a bit of a little girl at heart who lost her Mum when she was way too young to deal with it properly. Maybe this was part of how she dealt with it now by recreating that kind of little girl world. Tina had experienced a very different upbringing. She had two older brothers and a younger sister. Her parents had been great and she'd grown up in a happy home on one of the estates in Urmston. All her family had been supportive during recent days. Her Mum and Dad had wanted her to move back home but if she did that then the whole family thing would be so full on it would do her head in. So she'd settled for a dozen text messages every day, mainly from her Mum, plus a frequency of phone calls which sometimes never gave her a minute's peace. But she supposed that really made her a lucky girl compared to Andrea who never heard from her father and step-mother.

She glanced out of the window at the row of back gardens that were separated by a ginnel from the back gardens of the houses opposite. The mirror on Andrea's dressing table with its old fashioned regency style fittings was in front of what looked like a sliding door against the wall. That was strange, thought Tina. Why would you have a sliding door against a wall? She pulled it back and then she saw why. The wall was covered in pictures of James Clifton and Piers Jones. There were also pictures of Andrea on what looked like girls night's out with two girls she recognized as Sophie Cooper and Clarissa Dalton-Wood. She felt sick. What the fuck did all this mean? What had Andrea been up to? Was she responsible for these murders? Then she saw what made her retch. It was a series of pictures of her flat, about twenty of them, from the outside, from the street in both directions, and then there were twenty odd more of the inside, including the chest of drawers in the bedroom where the police had found the blood stained knives. How had Andrea got into her flat? She'd never given her a key. She heard her breathing turn into gasps of breath as if her body was reaching out and grabbing whatever air it could. She felt dizzy and light headed. She couldn't believe that Andrea could've deceived her in this way.

'What are you doing in my room?'

Tina turned round and saw Andrea standing in the doorway wrapped in a bathrobe. The look in her eyes almost freaked Tina out. It was like she was someone else.

'Andrea, what have you done?'

'I don't know what you're talking about'.

'Like fucking hell you don't! How have you got all these pictures of my flat?'

'That's none of your business and stop shouting'.

Tina was so terrified by the way Andrea was looking at her that she did as she was told and lowered her voice back down. 'It is my business, Andrea'

'You shouldn't be in here' said Andrea. She hadn't moved.

'You're being weird'.

'Deal with it'.

'What do you mean by that?'

'It's not my fault'.

'What isn't whose fault?'

'It's their fault'.

'Who? James Clifton? Piers Jones? Who are you talking about?' She started to cry. 'Andrea, did you set me up?'

'Why would you say that? I talked my grandmother into giving you a sanctuary'.

'But I didn't kill anyone'.

'No that's right. You didn't'.

'I didn't know you were friends with Sophie Cooper and Clarissa Dalton-Wood'

'And your point is?'

'Andrea … Andrea, I just don't know what to make of all this'.

Andrea stepped forward and closed the door behind her. 'You don't need to make anything of it'.

'But there you go again being all weird. Andrea, step aside and let me out'.

'I can't do that'.

'Andrea, step aside and let me fucking out!'

The first slap almost knocked Tina off her feet. She was going to have to fight to get herself out of this. But she wasn't prepared for the verbal onslaught Andrea was about to unleash on her.

'You stupid little fool' said Andrea, contemptuously. She then slapped her again. 'You really thought that I was going to take the blame? You who could pick men up whenever you felt like it compared to me who couldn't pick up a paper bag even on a good night. But people like me we hurt and we bleed. No fucker ever notices but we do. That's why we have to strike back'. She then gave Tina the back of her hand across her face.

Tina gasped with pain. She was shaking. If only she could make a dash for it to the door. 'Why did you use me in your little games?'

'Because I could and because you were there and because you suited our purposes'.

'But you made people think I'd murdered someone'.

'And now you know the truth even someone as stupid as you must know that I can't let you go now'.

Tina raised herself up and pushed Andrea out of the way before reaching for the door handle. She opened the door and was about to make it to freedom when Andrea grabbed her ankles and brought her down hard. Her face smashed against the wooden floor and the shock placed with the sudden onslaught of pain from the impact of hitting the floor gave Andrea valuable seconds. Tina was groaning on the edge of consciousness when Andrea came up and stamped hard on the back of Tina's neck. Then she did it again. It was enough to stun Tina into inaction. Then she stamped on Tina's neck a third time before leaning forward and yanking Tina's head back by grasping a clutch of her hair. She heard the sound of Tina's neck break. It was all over. Tina had paid for invading her privacy. It's never the right people who pay for the right crimes but that's just life.

Sharon Bellfield arranged to meet Brian and Helen Curzon at the Mayfair hotel on the premise that she was writing an article on the hotel industry in the northwest and how it was managing through the recession. Anita Patel wasn't on duty this particular morning but the delightful Tomas was and it struck Sharon how differently you look at a man after you've had him. As Tomas walked along and leant across reception to grab something from behind the desk Sharon recalled all the wonderful ways he'd used his body to please her. It was in the walk and the gestures of the man. She wouldn't need persuading if the offer came along to have him again. But for now, like Anita, she was in a relationship of platonic trust with Tomas. Like Anita, Tomas had divulged significant information to Sharon and she wasn't going to betray the trust of either of them. She'd checked and double-checked. The money she'd promised both of them had been transferred and received into their respective bank accounts. Anita was planning to return early to India and had used some of the money to change her flight back to Mumbai. Tomas was going to take Sharon's advice and move to London where he already had a friend, and set himself up as a male escort working entirely for himself. They'd both handed in their notices but of course Helen Curzon wouldn't know that Sharon knew that.

'Good morning' Helen Curzon gushed when she walked through from her office to greet her. 'You must be Sharon. I'm so pleased to meet you and I'm so glad you've decided to come out here and take an interest in our hotel. Please, come through to our lounge area. You are so welcome'.

Sharon wanted to be sick. This was going to be torture if this woman, who Sharon had already decided was beyond awful, carried on being as sickeningly sweet as this. But there was a bigger picture to think of here that made Sharon's squeamishness seem like a speck of dust on the floor.

'Thank you, Mrs. Curzon' said Sharon as she fell into step beside Helen Curzon.

'And please, please call me Helen. We don't go for formalities here and I want all our guests and visitors here at the Mayfair to feel as welcome as they would in my own home'.

Jesus, thought Sharon. How many layers of make-up had she plastered onto her face?

'Now I'm afraid my husband is rather unwell' said Helen. 'So I'm afraid he won't be joining us today'.

'That's a shame' said Sharon who had some serious questions for Mr. Curzon. 'Nothing serious I hope?'

'Oh no, just a cold but he's in that rather debilitating stage at the beginning of the infection when he can barely breathe'.

Sharon was disappointed that Brian Curzon wasn't going to show. She'd had everything worked out in her head as to how she was going to approach this but maybe it would be better with just Helen Curzon. However much Helen Curzon knew of her husband's affair with Anita Patel would be open for a jury to decide in due course if everything went to plan.

'Well I'm sorry to hear that' said Sharon.

They settled themselves in the far corner of the lounge in two high backed leather armchairs and with a small round table. Sharon had her recorder placed in the inside pocket of her jacket. She didn't want to risk Helen not agreeing to being taped. Helen then asked if Sharon would prefer tea or coffee and after she opted for coffee it was duly served. There was something strangely nostalgic about the place. It put Sharon in mind of all the games of running a house she used to play when she was a child.

'So how long have you owned this hotel, Helen?' Sharon began.

'Just over ten years' Helen replied. 'We've earned ourselves a formidable reputation in the area and indeed, further afield across the entire country and the continent too, we have regular guests staying with us from as far afield as Plymouth, Aberdeen, and Berlin. But we did take something of a knocking when the recession hit and we were just coming out of that when recent events took us back'.

'You mean the discovery of the body of James Clifton behind the main hotel building?'

'Yes' Helen confirmed. 'It was a dreadfully unfortunate thing for the young man and his family of course but it did lead to several cancellations from our forward bookings when word got out across the press. We still have a police presence too as you saw when you came in to the hotel. They say it's necessary but it has been several days now'.

'What do you think could've happened there?'

'Sharon, I really don't want to talk about the whole James Clifton situation. It's bad enough it happened at all without prolonging the awful agony'.

'And does your husband feel the same?'

'Well of course' Helen replied a little indignantly. 'Brian and I have been as one on everything since the day we met'.

Interesting, thought Sharon. They went on to talk about the hotel business in general and about what specific marketing strategies the Curzon's were going to employ to win back some of the business they'd lost. Everything Helen mentioned was legitimate but Sharon was getting impatient. Enough of luring the old bag into a false sense of security. It was time to stick the knife in and make her bleed.

'Okay' she said. 'So I'm a business woman from out of town and I have meetings to attend and contracts to negotiate and so on and so forth. What can I get here at the Mayfair that would make me choose it above any of the other hotels in the area?'

'You'd get all the comforts of home but with the style of a modern boutique like hotel and a level of service on a par with anything that any of the larger hotels in any European city can offer'.

'Except that you're in the middle of the suburbs of Stockport here and a fair distance from the centre of Manchester'.

'Well that's true in terms of basic geography but we certainly feel close to the big hotels in Manchester because of our attitude which is international and sophisticated'.

'I'm sure' said Sharon. 'So as a businesswoman from out of town who's here to negotiate contracts and so on and so forth, what would that level of service look like to me?'

'Well my staff would give you all the personal and individual attention they could and they'd make sure you left here feeling happy that you spent your money here with us and not anywhere else'.

'And what about sex?'

Helen looked like she'd stuck her wet finger into an electric socket. 'I beg your pardon?'

'What if I wanted to buy sex during my stay?'

'Miss Bellfield, I can assure you that we don't run that kind of establishment'.

'No you can't give me that assurance at all' Sharon countered. 'You know it and I know it. You use half your staff here as prostitutes but I'm sure it's not in their job description'.

'This is absurd! I don't know what the hell you're talking about'.

'This hotel has been going downhill financially for months now' said Sharon who couldn't make up her mind whether or not Helen Curzon was complicit or innocent in the workings of evil that have spun round this hotel. 'You and your husband Brian wanted a way out of your financial predicament and a way out of your business association with Bernie Connelly'.

'Where did you get this scurrilous information?'

'Various sources' said Sharon.

'Well when I find out who they are they'll be hearing from my solicitor'.

'I wouldn't take on cases you won't win if I was you'.

'You're out of your mind'.

'This will be the first and only chance you get to tell your story to us, Helen' said Sharon. 'I'm trying to help you if you'd only see it. I'm a lot kinder than some of my colleagues from some of the national papers so why don't you talk to me?'

'You tricked me into thinking you were going to help me promote my business!'

'But you don't want to promote your business'.

'What do you mean?'

'Come on, Helen. I just don't believe your cry of innocence. You and Brian have been out to damage the hotel's reputation to the point where you'd be able to sell the property to a developer. I know you've been running it into the ground so that you'd get to the point where you would have to sell it. And all because you want out of the arrangement you found yourselves in with none other than Bernie Connelly, one of Manchester's most notorious gangsters and who runs a prostitution ring that includes the Mayfair. So, let's get real, Helen. Was the dumping of the body of James Clifton such an inconvenience to you? Or was it a deliberate act that you were fully aware of because you know who killed him?

'You need to tell us everything, Melanie' said Jeff who was losing patience with being given the runaround by this lot. 'And I mean everything'.

Melanie Cartwright began singing like the proverbial canary once she acknowledged that she was in serious trouble. She had her brief sitting beside her but Jeff and Rebecca both noted that he wasn't doing anything to stop her confession. Her hands were shaking that much she couldn't even hold her glass of water.

'I couldn't believe it when I walked into the crew room on the day of my first flight with the airline and Sophie Cooper was standing there. She looked straight into my eyes like she always used to. She and Clarissa Dalton-Wood made my life absolute hell when I was in my last year at school and they joined my class. They were rotten to me. They had it in for me from the start'.

'What did the school do about that?' asked Rebecca.

'I told them what was happening but they did nothing' said Melanie, tearfully. She was playing with a paper tissue, ripping bits off it and letting them fall into her hand. 'But you see, those bitches were clever. They never did anything that would be obvious to other people but they used whispers that nobody else could hear and physical assaults when nobody else was around. Then they started getting at me on the way to and from school and they even hung around near my house at weekends. In the end I thought I couldn't be safe anywhere'.

'Were you friends with Andrea Kay?'

'Yes I was' said Melanie. 'But Sophie and Clarissa even put paid to that'.

'How so, Melanie?'

'They somehow managed to make Andrea a friend of theirs. They subjected her to the same treatment as me at the start but she gave in and became their kind of enforcer. If they wanted someone intimidating they got Andrea to do it. If they wanted someone beaten up then they got Andrea to do it. Andrea was a very needy girl, you know. Her mother had died, her father had fucked off with another woman who made it clear she didn't want Andrea to be part of their lives and she went to live with her grandma. She needed to belong. She needed to be needed by someone. She was easy prey for the likes of Sophie Cooper and Clarissa Dalton-Wood who gave her all that but only at the cost of her doing their dirty work for them. She was stupid. She should never have gone along with them'.

'So Melanie, did the bullying stop when you all finished school?' Jeff wondered.

'Well yes until I met up with Sophie again at work' said Melanie with the tears still rolling down her face. 'My Mum and Dad will be so disappointed in me when they hear about what I've done'.

'And what exactly have you done, Melanie?'

Melanie was sobbing her heart out. 'I went into work for Sophie that night. I didn't know it was because she wanted to do something to her fiancé. I swear I didn't know anything about that. But as soon as I saw Sophie was working there too I knew it wouldn't be long before she came knocking. She said I owed them, you see. Years ago, she said that one day she'd be in a position to ask me to repay the debt'.

'And what debt was that, Melanie?' Rebecca asked.

'I was pregnant' she wailed. 'I wasn't even sixteen but Sophie and Clarissa said they knew someone who could do something about it'.

'You mean you had an abortion?'

'Yes' Melanie admitted. Her tears were flowing so much now that her face was soaked. 'They knew this doctor who would do it without asking any questions and they took me to him. I was desperate for them not to tell Andrea Kay because although she'd gone over to their side I still considered her to be something of a friend of mine'.

'So why didn't you want to tell her about your pregnancy?'

'Because of who the father was!'

'And who was it?'

'Andrea's father! Brian Curzon was the father of my baby. I'd been sleeping with him for six months before I got pregnant'.

'Get Brian Curzon in here!' Jeff ordered from the middle of the crowded squad room after he and Rebecca had finished interviewing Melanie Cartwright. 'Arrest him on the charge of having sex with a girl who was underage and we'll take it from there. Where the hell were Melanie Cartwright's parents at that time? Didn't they notice their fifteen-year old daughter was pregnant? God save us from these useless individuals who have children.

'Sir?' Rebecca ventured holding up a file.

'What?'

'Clarissa Dalton-Wood? She's next to be interviewed?'

'Ah yes, another one of our poor little rich girls who took great delight in being sadistic bullies. Ollie, any news on Andrea Kay?'

'No, sir' Ollie replied. 'She's not at work and there's nobody answering the door at home'.

'Well get a warrant and break your way in' Jeff ordered. 'Do a thorough search of her belongings and when you find her, I want her down here as quickly as possible. Also Ollie, dig out that piece of footage from the CCTV of the Manchester Hilton three years ago on the night Kim Barnes was murdered'.

'Of the woman dressed in black, sir?'

'That's it. I think if we take a closer and now, more informed look, we'll see that it's Andrea Kay. So now to Miss Dalton-Wood. Let's see how she's going to try and lie her way out of trouble because she will do. Just how many more layers on this case have we got to get through before we finally get to the truth?'

'Which is?'

'That Andrea Kay is the killer of James Clifton, Piers Jones, and Malcolm Barnes, and I think Kim Barnes three years ago. It all makes perfect sense now, Becky, and like I said before, we've got to get just one of them to crack and the chain will be broken'.

'And Brian Curzon?'

'Well we know he's a pervert and we now know that he's Andrea Kay's father. So I'm sure it won't be long before something else pops up out of the box about him'.

Like most girls from backgrounds like that of the Dalton-Wood family, Clarissa sat in the interview room with the most defiant look on her face, an expensive lawyer at her side, and an attitude that informed the rest of the human race that they were all beneath her. Her natural blond hair was tied back in a bun and she wore a long pink coat over a short black dress. She was a very pretty girl, Jeff noted. Green eyes and a small narrow mouth but not a lot of make-up as far as he could see. She didn't need it.

'How did you get her to do it?' Jeff opened.

There was a pause and then Clarissa said 'How did I get who to do what?'

'How did you get Andrea Kay to murder for you?'

The lawyer butted in and told Jeff that his client would not be answering such direct and leading questions as that had been.

'It must've been difficult for you'.

'What must've been?'

'Well there you were down at Grange Park surrounded by the beauty of rural Somerset and communities of horse riding country folk and then you're pulled back up to sunny old Manchester and thrown into what some would call a bog standard comprehensive in a northern suburb where you're surrounded by types you wouldn't normally associate with in a million years. So how did you handle it? You decided to pick on the two most vulnerable girls, Andrea Kay and Melanie Cartwright, bully them, humiliate them, knock them off their pedestals and then draw them into your sordid, murderous little games'.

Clarissa smirked. 'You must be some kind of fantasist'.

'Oh we have a sworn statement from Melanie Cartwright telling us everything'.

'Then why do you need me here?'

'Because there are gaps in the story that she couldn't fill'.

'Such as?'

'Well how did you feel when you found out that your late fiancé Piers Jones was having an affair with Annette Bryson?'

Clarissa shifted a little in her seat. It was the first indication from this Ice Queen that she may not be quite as sure of herself as she first seemed.

'It was his life' she answered. 'If he wanted to waste it on her when he already had me then that was his decision'.

'Did you know Annette Bryson was pregnant?'

'Of course I knew'.

'And how did you react when you found that out?'

'I was very upset as a matter of fact' Clarissa admitted. 'You see, I can't have children. I have a problem with my reproductive system'.

'I'm sorry to hear that'.

'What's it to you?'

'A lot if your jealousy drove you to have him murdered'.

The lawyer stepped in again with another warning to Jeff that he would instruct his client not to make any further comment if this line of questioning continued.

'Oh I'm so sorry' said Jeff. 'I thought I was just doing my job'.

'You don't have anything of a case' scoffed Clarissa.

'I'll be the judge of that, Miss Dalton-Wood'.

'It's interesting, Miss Dalton-Wood' said Rebecca, taking over from Jeff. 'To note that you haven't mentioned one word of sorrow at the passing of your fiancé? It's only a couple of days but there are no tears and yet this was the man you were set to spend the rest of your life with'.

Clarissa shrugged. 'We all deal with these things in our own way' she said. 'I do my crying alone. I don't make a public show of it'.

'How very controlled'.

'Call it what the hell you like'.

'It might help to convince others of your innocence if you did show some emotion'.

'Let me spell this out to you' said Clarissa. 'I have nothing to convince anyone of. Got it? Absolutely nothing so the sooner you let me out of this awful place the sooner I can convince my father not to make representations to the chief Constable about you. They're friends, you see. They play golf together and have drinks parties'.

'And that's of relevance to this case because?'

'I'm just letting you know that my family is well connected'.

'Well that won't stop us from charging you with conspiracy to murder if we see you have a case to answer' said Jeff. 'No matter who your friends are'.

'Oh how very … left-wing of you to think that connections in higher society are there to be broken. Thank God I'm more of a realist'.

'Meaning?'

'That you don't have the first idea of how to communicate across class'.

Jeff's blood was starting to boil. 'Oh is that right?'

'Yes it is' Clarissa insisted. 'I had nothing whatsoever to do with the murder of Piers'.

'You're lying' said Rebecca.

'Prove it!'

'Oh we will' said Jeff. 'I'm terminating this interview at 1521 but it's only the start of questioning for you. We'll be back'.

Ollie Wright had been working so hard on the case that he hadn't even noticed all the blatant manipulation that was going on behind his back and orchestrated by Jonathan Freeman. The whole squad was busy but Freeman still managed to play his games like his life depended on it. He was listening to one of the other police officers who was telling him about his opposition to the recent change in the law allowing gay marriage. They were standing behind a temporary partition in the office and Freeman knew that Ollie Wright, sitting at his desk but out of sight of where Freeman was with the other police officer, would be able to hear the other officer but might struggle to hear Freeman because the photocopying machine was between them and that made a rather loud noise.

'Well that was an interesting conversation' said Freeman when he returned to his desk opposite Ollie. 'You know where you stand with that guy'.

Ollie decided to try and not rise to Freeman's goading. He was too busy and too knackered to get into it with him now.

'Sorry, mate, but am I invisible or something?' Freeman went on.

Ollie sighed. 'What?'

'Well I spoke to you and you didn't have the courtesy to reply'.

'I'm busy, Jonathan. Just what is it you want?'

'Well a little courtesy and respect might be good' said Jonathan. 'I did stick up for you the other day with the boss, remember?'

'For which I was grateful and told you so'.

'Well, you've got a great way of showing it' said Jonathan, under his breath.

'What did you just say?'

'Annette Bryson' said Jonathan. 'Hooked herself a nice white man who then went and got himself murdered. You blacks don't have much luck when you try and integrate with the more accepted part of society, do you mate? Hope you have better luck with your white man'.

'Alright, that's enough!'

Jonathan made it look like he'd been totally taken by surprise with Ollie's reaction to his taunting. 'Sorry, mate. Are you ashamed of who you are?'

'I've never been ashamed of who I am'.

'Is that why you keep that copy of Gay Times hidden away in your top drawer instead of on top of your desk for everyone to see?'

'I do not keep … ' Ollie stopped and opened the top drawer of his desk. And there was a copy of Gay Times. Freeman must've planted it there. 'What have I ever done to you?'

'You're alive' Freeman snarled. 'That's enough'.

'Okay, that's it! I'm going to make a formal complaint against you'.

'Oh well be my guest' said Freeman who then stood up. 'Because I relish the chance of telling everyone that you, DC Ollie Wright, are nothing more than an anti-Semitic bully. That's right, mate, I'm Jewish. And you are so going to regret taking me on'.

FIREFLIES EIGHTEEN

The last thing Jeff needed to deal with was the official complaint of anti-Semitism brought by Jonathan Freeman against Ollie Wright. The timing was lousy in the extreme but it was made even worse by the fact that Jeff didn't believe for one second that Ollie was in any way anti-Semitic. He'd interviewed Freeman himself on the basis of a background check carried out by human resources. Freeman had come across well at that interview and Jeff had been keen to get the kind of help for Ollie that Freeman could provide. Maybe he should've checked on the extent of that background check and seen through what he now saw as Freeman's act.

'We have to follow this through, Jeff' said chief Superintendent Geraldine Chambers who'd called Jeff to her office to discuss the matter.

'I don't believe Freeman's allegations, ma'am'.

'And I accept your judgment, Jeff' said Chambers. 'But Freeman is adamant that Ollie Wright subjected him to a constant and unrelenting barrage of anti-Semitic abuse and he feels particularly aggrieved as he claims to have been wholly and utterly supportive of Wright's homosexuality'.

'Well at the risk of repeating myself, ma'am, I just don't buy any of this' said Jeff. 'Firstly, DC Wright is one of my most trusted and valuable officers and I can certainly back up my claims with facts. Second, this is calling into question the professional ethics of DC Wright which is something I simply cannot accept, ma'am'.

'I understand your feelings, Jeff' said Chambers. 'Really I do. You're standing by one of your officers and I understand that more than most, believe me, because I've had occasion to do the same in the past. But that doesn't change the fact that an official complaint has been made and it has to be followed up'.

'Can we at least put it on hold until after this investigation is concluded, ma'am?' asked an exasperated Jeff. 'I've got suspects in custody with the clock ticking on whether I have to either charge them or release them, two more who we're out there searching for, and one, Melanie Cartwright, who let herself be bullied by two of the most manipulative young women I've ever come across. Freeman knows all that very well and I'm angry that he's chosen this time. Ma'am, this is attention seeking of the worst order'.

'You may be right'.

'I believe I am'.

'The case you're dealing with is complicated'.

'You're telling me, ma'am'.

'And do you have any conclusions at this point?'

'Ma'am, Sophie Cooper and Clarissa Dalton-Wood somehow used Andrea Kay to commit murder on their behalf. What's still open to debate in my mind is how far Andrea Kay's father, Brian Curzon, was involved in the killings, and how far the reach of the murders goes back to our old friend Bernie Connelly'.

'The man who you're convinced had your friend Andy Kirkpatrick killed?'

'Yes, ma'am. I'm not saying this is some kind of personal crusade that risks blinding me to the truth. But let's just say that if we are able to nail Connelly then I will be personally very satisfied'.

'How's Ollie, sir?' Rebecca asked as she and Jeff made their way down to the interview rooms.

'Not entirely surprised' said Jeff who'd been trying to damp down the uproar that Jonathan Freeman's allegations against Ollie Wright had caused. The squad room was on fire with it all. 'He'd had the feeling that Freeman was cooking something up against him. He's now made a counter charge of racism against Freeman who now contends that because the squad are all lined up behind Ollie then there's some kind of anti-Semitic conspiracy going on. It's added power to his cause. He's going to the press with it all. This is not going to look good'.

'How do you think it feels for me? I was sleeping with Freeman'.

Jeff felt a rush of embarrassment before asking. 'Did you have any idea of his feelings?'

'I had a feeling that Freeman held certain prejudices but I shrugged it off' said Rebecca who was ashamed of the way she'd turned a blind eye to Jonathan Freeman's obvious racism. She shouldn't have let sex get in the way of that. 'I didn't really give it any serious thought to be honest'.

'Well now is the time to think about it seriously because you'll need to tell what you know to Chief Superintendent Chambers' said Jeff. 'Maybe we can head off an official enquiry and Ollie can get out from under the shadow Freeman has placed over him'.

'Ollie is no anti-Semite, sir'.

'Of course he isn't' said Jeff. 'And one way or another we'll prove that. But for now let's get to Sophie Cooper. I want results and conclusions and I want them today'.

Rebecca wasn't quite sure how to read Sophie Cooper. She was some ways defiant, some ways contrite, some ways looking for any excuse to get herself out of trouble. She was a complicated picture but no more so than either she or Jeff had dealt with before.

'My client is prepared to do a deal, detective' said Barbara Matthews, Sophie Cooper's brief. 'She will tell you everything she knows about the murder of both James Clifton and Piers Jones in return for immunity from prosecution'.

No chance, thought Jeff. 'I'd like to hear what your client has to say first before I agree to any deal. DS Stockton?'

'Sophie, what happened after you switched ID cards with Melanie Cartwright and left your crew reporting centre on the night of the murder of James Clifton?'

Sophie took a deep breath. 'I needed justice for the way James had betrayed me. I was possessed by this need to get my own back. Clarissa was waiting for me outside and I got into the car with her and headed to her place. I got changed there and then we sat and waited for a call from Andrea. Andrea had two phones, one that she used for normal stuff and one that she used for other things'.

'Why was Andrea Kay doing all this for you?'

Sophie smirked. 'When Clarissa and I were sent to Willowbrook comprehensive she was desperate to be friends with us. We accepted that because we saw her as someone we could use'.

'Did she murder Kim Barnes in the Manchester Hilton three years ago?'

Sophie took a deep breath. 'Yes' she said.

'At your instigation?'

'Yes again' Sophie answered with a sideways glance at her lawyer. 'I felt very betrayed by Malcolm. I wanted him to suffer and to cry as many tears as I had when he dumped me for that bitch. I wanted revenge but I didn't just want to get even. I wanted to go further. I really wanted him to feel such intense pain for the rest of his life for having dared to betray me. So the three of us, Clarissa, Andrea, and me came up with the plan to rip his wedding night apart. I felt right about doing it. That may sound abhorrent to you but it's what I needed'.

'So tell us what happened with James Clifton, Sophie?'

'Look, am I going to get my immunity or what?'

'I don't think you're in a position to call the shots, Sophie' said Jeff. 'You've already confessed to conspiracy to murder in the case of Kim Barnes and you've implicated two other people. Now carry on with what you have to tell us and then I'll decide on what happens next'.

'I just want this over with'.

'Then carry on talking and don't stop until you've told us everything we need to know' said Jeff. 'And don't even think of playing any games with us'.

'Games! You think I'm just playing games?'

'We don't know all of what you were doing yet, Sophie' said Rebecca, firmly. She was surprised by how easily Sophie Cooper was capitulating. There was a look of disturbance on her face that was holding down her usual defiance. 'We haven't got all the answers we need from you yet, not by a long stretch'.

Sophie exchanged whispers with her lawyer briefly before continuing.

'Okay .... '

' ... the night of the murder of James Clifton if you wouldn't mind, Sophie?'

'Alright, I'm getting there!' snapped Sophie.

'That's better' said Rebecca.

'What do you mean by that?'

'Well we're not used to Sophie Cooper being so quiet and reasonable' said Rebecca. 'Usually she's like a tiger with no teeth'.

'Oh that's it, belittle me. You lot are so good at doing that'.

'Just get back to the matter in hand, Sophie' said Jeff.

'I kept Andrea apart from all my other friends and so she could be close to James and report back to Clarissa and me. Then we got a message from her that Tina Webb was taking James home. I screamed out with anger. I hated James at that moment and I couldn't believe the same thing was happening to me again that happened with Malcolm all those years ago. What is it with me and stag nights? That's how I lost Malcolm to Kim and that's how I saw red when it came to James'. She started to cry. 'We, that's Clarissa and me, drove round to Tina Webb's place and waited nearby in the car. A little while later we were joined by Andrea and then we saw James and Tina arrive in a taxi. They went into her flat and we waited again. As you can imagine it was pretty painful for me. Then James came out on his own and Andrea went up to him. I don't know what she said but she got him into her car where she administered the rohipnol. Then she drove off and that was the last I saw of her or James that night'.

'Did you actually discuss murdering James with Andrea?'

'Andrea knew that I couldn't take James cheating on me again. I wanted him dead for sure and I knew that Andrea would take care of that for me'.

'Just like that?' said Rebecca.

'He cheated on me and I didn't deserve it! I owed him nothing but he deserved to pay'.

'Most people would've just ended the relationship and moved on' said Rebecca who couldn't mistake the look of absolute hatred in Sophie's eyes. She was certainly the jealous type alright.

'Yes' said Sophie who was wiping her face with a tissue. 'Well I'm not most people and I believe in getting my own back'.

'With murder?'

'If necessary' said Sophie. 'Sometimes people have to be taught a lesson they'll never forget'.

'Is that a little bit of home spun philosophy from your brother Bernie?' Jeff wanted to know.

'Leave my brother out of this'.

Jeff leaned forward and rested his clasped hands and forearms on the desk. 'Well come on, Sophie, all this confession is very useful but let's get down to what's really going on here. Where did Andrea Kay get the rohipnol from?'

'I have no idea'.

'I don't believe you'.

'Are you calling me a liar?'

'Yes, that's exactly what I'm calling you' said Jeff. 'Are you really trying to convince us that you had no part in either the murder of James Clifton or Piers Jones except for identifying them to Andrea Kay?'

'That is the truth, yes' Sophie insisted.

'And Malcolm Barnes? Were you behind his murder as well?'

'I swear to God I knew nothing about that and if you don't believe me then ask yourself why I would confess to everything else and not that?'

'Everybody has their limitations and yours is when it comes to the truth' Jeff went on. 'You give us so much but you don't give us it all. I think your brother not only supplied the rohipnol but provided you, Clarissa Dalton-Wood and Andrea Kay with the support of every kind you needed to carry out your evil deeds'.

'You've got a trip wire in your head when it comes to my brother'.

'So convince me otherwise?'

'You've got all of this so very wrong'.

'Oh is that right?'

'What did you do after Andrea Kay drove off with a drugged James Clifton in her car, Sophie?' asked Rebecca.

'We went back to Clarissa's place and broke open a bottle of champagne'.

Jeff and Rebecca looked at each other and shook their heads.

'And you pretended to all the world like you were so distraught' said Jeff.

Sophie shrugged her shoulders. 'Wouldn't you in the circumstances?'

'Were you present on the night Piers Jones was lured away, presumably by Andrea, and murdered?'

'Yes' said Sophie. 'It happened more or less the same way as with James. He came out of Annette Bryson's flat and Andrea used whatever charms she has to get him into her car'.

'And neither you nor Clarissa saw Piers or Andrea again that night?'

'No, we didn't'.

'Whose idea was it to try and blame Tina Webb for Clifton's murder, Sophie?'

'Andrea's' said Sophie. 'Clarissa and me just told Andrea what we wanted her to do and she just did it in the best way she saw fit. She was like a puppy. A stupid, obedient little puppy'.

'Who would even kill for you'.

'That's about it, yes' Sophie confirmed.

FIREFLIES NINETEEN

'It looks like she struggled' said June Hawkins, the pathologist who was crouched down over the body of Tina Webb which was still halfway out of Andrea Kay's bedroom door. 'Her neck is broken but there are marks on the back of her neck and at the top of her back. I think she's been hit with something or had something pushed up against her neck and then pressure applied. She must've been terrified in those last few moments'.

'I don't think we need to draw up a list of suspects' said Jeff. 'This is Andrea Kay's work'.

'And Tina Webb must've been bloody angry with her if she'd found out that someone she thought was her friend had in fact set her up for murder' said Rebecca.

'Well Andrea Kay clearly got the better of her' said Jeff. 'Just like she's got the better of us all this time'.

'You should get a lot from all that lot' said June, gesturing her head towards all the pictures and clippings from Andrea Kay's 'secret' wall behind the lockable screen.

'Discovering that was probably what got Tina Webb killed' said Jeff.

'So you've charged Sophie Cooper and Clarissa Dalton-Wood I understand?' June asked.

'Yes and you should've seen the commotion' said Jeff. 'Sophie Cooper completely lost it. She started screaming and then she tried to lift one of the chairs and throw it at us. Clarissa Dalton-Wood was a little better but she couldn't begin to imagine how a poor little rich girl like her could possibly be placed in a standard cell'.

'Like there's a non standard cell?' June questioned with a smile on her face.

'Exactly' said Rebecca.

Jeff was satisfied that they were reaching the end of investigations into the murders of James Clifton and Piers Jones. But then there were the murders of Malcolm Barnes and now Tina Webb. There was something occupying his subconscious that was making him restless. Everything was pointing at Andrea Kay. But what if they were wrong?

'We need to talk to Andrea's grandmother' said Jeff.

'She's sitting in the lounge' Rebecca explained. 'She found the body when she came home from shopping and not surprisingly she's pretty upset'.

Rebecca followed Jeff downstairs where he pulled up a stool and sat next to Andrea's grandmother, Marjorie Kay.

'Mrs. Kay, I'm really sorry to have to ask you this' Jeff began, his voice and manner as gentle as he could make them. 'But did you have any idea of what your granddaughter was up to?'

'No' Marjorie answered, swallowing her tears and staring into space. 'She was such a sweet child. She had her dolls and her toys. My daughter was a good mother but her heart was broken by her husband Brian. I could bloody well swing for that man. He destroyed my daughter's life and now he's destroyed my granddaughter's too'.

'How has he destroyed Andrea's life, Mrs. Kay?' Jeff asked, gently.

'By marrying that bitch of a woman Helen he made a choice between her and Andrea. She never got over it. She must've been driven mad by the sense of betrayal. Oh God I should've known! I never asked why she kept her bedroom door locked even from me. I indulged her. I over compensated for what she'd lost and it's led to all this'. She started to weep. 'A lovely young girl like Tina dies in my house and my Andrea … I've lived here over fifty years. My late husband and I brought up Andrea's mother here and this is where I gave Andrea sanctuary when she couldn't live with her step-mother anymore'.

'Mrs. Kay, none of this is your fault' said Jeff, gently. 'You mustn't blame yourself'.

'Then who is to blame? Somebody has to be'.

'When we find your granddaughter we may be able to find the answer to that, Mrs. Kay' said Rebecca. 'Have you any idea where she might have gone?'

'No' said Marjorie, crying unstoppable tears. 'I've known my granddaughter for all of her years on this earth and yet now I understand I don't know her at all'.

'Mrs. Kay?' asked Jeff. 'What is the relationship like between Andrea and her father now?'

'Well … they don't see each other as far as I know but maybe that's something else she's kept behind my back. I've looked after her all these years … I just can't understand why she's acted the way she's done'.

'What about her relationship with her step-mother Helen?'

'Oh that's a relationship that will never heal' said Marjorie. 'Andrea blames Helen for the death of her mother and so do I. It was Helen's affair with Brian that caused the heartbreak that led my daughter, Andrea's mother, to commit suicide'.

'Could you think of a situation where the relationship could be repaired?' Jeff went on.

'No' said Marjorie, firmly. 'But like I say, I never thought my granddaughter would be capable of killing someone so don't quote me on anything'.

Jeff and Rebecca got back to the squad room and Jeff was consumed with the idea that they were looking in the wrong place.

'Sir?' said Ollie. 'I've just had the editor of the Manchester Evening Chronicle on the line. He said that a journalist of theirs, Sharon Bellfield, went to interview Brian and Helen Curzon at the Mayfair hotel two days ago'.

'And?'

'She was supposed to file her copy on the interview straight after but they haven't heard from her since, there's no answer at her flat and her mobile is going straight to voicemail, sir. She wasn't due any leave and the editor has checked with her family. They haven't heard from her either'.

Jeff stood and thought for a moment and then said 'Alright, people, this is what we're going to do. DS Stockton and myself will lead a squad of uniformed officers to the Mayfair hotel to bring Helen Curzon in for questioning. All the way through this investigation we've known that if Andrea Kay is our killer then she must've had help, right?'

'But it can't have been Helen Curzon, sir' Rebecca reasoned. 'Andrea Kay detests her step-mother'.

'That's true' said Jeff. 'But I think Helen Curzon will give us the final answers. Don't ask me why. Just go with me'.

Just before they were about to leave for the Curzon home another call came through. This time it was from Anita Patel, former employee of the Curzon's at the Mayfair hotel, who was calling from Mumbai with information she'd told to the reporter from the Manchester Evening Chronicle but which she thought she really ought to tell to the police.

Andrea Kay had already administered the rohipnol drug to her father Brian. She'd stripped him naked and was getting ready to relieve him of his manhood.

'You really don't feel anything for him, do you' said Helen who was standing behind Andrea in the lounge of her house out on the edge of the Saddleworth moors.

'Do you?'

Helen turned her eyes to the view out of the window. It was possible to see the two counties of Derbyshire and Yorkshire plus the start of the urban conurbation of Greater Manchester but that's not what was occupying her thoughts today. She and Brian had bought the place when she thought nothing would be able to offer even the remotest threat to their happiness. But that joy had been soured. Anita Patel was just the latest in a long line of affairs that Brian had humiliated her with. And yet she'd done everything for him. She'd brought out the best in him and restored his confidence after that miserable bitch of his first wife had sucked all the joy out of his soul. She'd worked night and day building up the business and making sure they had a future. Then Brian had risked it all by going into business with that evil crook Bernie Connelly. They'd brought prostitution into the Mayfair. How fucking dare they! She'd wanted to establish a legitimate business and that's what she had done. Brian and his friend had ruined everything. She knew that the only reason they were experiencing a high occupancy rate was because of the 'other' services they offered and that's why she'd agreed to Andrea's little plan. If she could do something to damage the reputation of the business to the extent that it couldn't even survive as a glorified knocking shop then she and

Brian could cut their losses and sell from under the nose of Bernie Connelly. They could've then added what money they did make to what they would've made from selling the house and then bought something on the continent right away from everything. But then she'd discovered Brian's affair with Anita Patel and something had snapped inside her. She ran out of strength to keep up the brave face. It was over.

'We're more alike than you'd like to think, you and I' said Helen as she watched her step-daughter meticulously prepare her act of savagery.

'How do you make that out?'

'We're both intense characters' said Helen. 'We don't forgive or forget'.

Andrea had been happy to work with her step-mother whilst it was expedient. But she still hated the sight of Helen even though she'd been useful. It had been a strange set of circumstances that had brought them together. Helen had realised that the female in black who the police had been looking for after the murder of Kim Barnes in the Manchester Hilton had been Andrea. She'd confronted Andrea who'd admitted to what she'd done but Helen had promised not to inform on her if Andrea promised to help her out with something that would be beyond the law if she ever needed it. She'd made up her mind that one more affair and she would have Brian killed. It was no idle threat she'd made to him. But he'd callously dismissed her feelings and jumped into bed with Anita Patel. That's when she called in the favour from her step-daughter. She knew she'd be able to use Andrea's hatred for her father as a weapon to get her onboard.

'Do you want me to wait until he's coming to?' asked Andrea.

'Yes'

'You really want him to know what I'm going to do to him?'

'Yes'

'You must hate him as much as I do'.

'Yes, I think I probably do'.

'I'm getting revenge for my mother'.

'I'm getting revenge for myself'.

'You had nothing but contempt for my mother'.

'Do you really want to do this now?'

Andrea walked up to her. 'Maybe we could've been friends?'

Helen gave a half-smile. 'I somehow doubt that'.

Helen turned to walk towards the kitchen when Andrea lunged at her and stabbed her in the back. Helen felt the air escape her lungs as she fell to her knees and Andrea then stabbed her again but this time in the neck. The blood was pouring out everywhere.

'That was also for my mother'.

.

'I wanted to kill' said Andrea. 'I wanted someone else to feel the pain that I'd always felt. I wanted them to go through all of what I'd gone through. Because you see, nobody ever said sorry to me. Nobody ever helped me dry my tears. Nobody tried to understand what I was feeling'.

'And what was that, Andrea?'

'My Mum had left me. My Dad had taken up with another woman who hated me'.

'And how did that make you feel?'

'Lost' said Andrea. 'Abandoned by my own parents'.

'But you went to live with your Gran?'

'Yes but we never talked about anything' said Andrea. 'She and my Granddad looked after me but the care was all about putting a roof over my head with food on the table and clean sheets on the bed. They never really took an interest in me as an individual person'.

'And that upset you?'

'I just wanted somebody to say sorry for all that I'd lost. But nobody did'.

'So what happened when you met Sophie and Clarissa?'

'Oh they were so glamourous compared to all the rest of us' Andrea recalled. 'But I was never really part of anything at school. I was a loner. I didn't really fit in anywhere. I only had Melanie as a friend and she was another misfit who nobody else wanted to be around. Then Sophie and Clarissa took a shine to me. They wanted to make me their friend'.

'They wanted to use you'.

'No, it wasn't like that!'

'Okay, Andrea, keep calm'.

'They were my friends' she insisted. 'They were the only ones, the only ones who even noticed I was there so don't you dare say that they were only using me'.

'Did they ask you to kill Kim Barnes on her wedding night?'

'She deserved it' said Andrea. 'She'd taken Malcolm away from Sophie and she deserved to get hers. I was happy to do it for Sophie'.

'Why didn't she do it herself?'

'Because that's what you do for your friends' Andrea explained as if she was telling how she wouldn't let her friend drive her car if she was drunk. 'You're there for them and you help them when someone has caused them pain and isn't sorry for it'.

'Like your father had done to you?'

'Yes' said Andrea. 'There's too much of that, far too much of it. People cause pain and hurt and heartache to others and they don't care about the consequences. They never say sorry. They couldn't give a shit and they just get away with it. I was sick of seeing all that keep on happening. I wanted to do something to put things right. I wanted people to get their own back and I started with my friends'.

'How did your step-mother help you with the murders of James Clifton and Piers Jones?'

'Helen organized for me to have a room at the Mayfair where I took James. I said I'd do anything he wanted sexually even though I've never slept with a man in my life. Helen said I could take him in through a back way at a spot where the CCTV cameras don't cover. I gave him the rohipnol in a glass of wine and then once he was under I castrated him. I dumped the body between the rubbish bins. Back in the room Helen and I cleaned it up although there was little mess. I was very careful that way. Then the next day she closed the room off for renovation'.

'And Piers Jones?'

'I offered him a swig from a bottle of water I had in my car and into which I'd put the rohipnol' Andrea revealed. 'I drove out to the house at Saddleworth, my father was on night duty at the Mayfair that night, and took the body into the garage. That's where I castrated him but it was my idea to sit him under that tree in the village where his stupid bitch of a mother lived. That was genius. I wanted to teach that Paula a lesson good and fucking proper. She'd taken my promotion off me and wasn't sorry'.

'You make it all sound so easy'.

'It is when you're determined. We chose their stag nights because they're supposed to be a celebration and we wanted to ruin it. And because it all started on the stag night Malcolm Barnes had when he got off with the Kim bitch. James was easiest to lure away. Most men think with their dicks at the best of times and when they've had a few they're even worse. They'd even shag someone like me when they've had a few. Piers was more difficult. I had to say I had car trouble and make a joke about being a useless female. He was quite sweet really but he was still being unfaithful to poor Clarissa'.

'You said someone like you?'

'Well I'm not exactly a catwalk model or anything. I don't look like any of those girls you see in the magazines who get all the men with all the money. I'm not like Tina'.

'What do you mean, Andrea?'

'Well she could click her fingers and get a man just like that. And she didn't even care about any of them. It was all just sex to her'.

'Tina was your friend, Andrea. Why did you try and set her up?'

'She was in the wrong place at the wrong time'.

'In your statement to the police you admit that you planted evidence in her flat, Andrea. That was a deliberate act that could've seen her go away to prison'.

Andrea looked down and for the first time showed what could be described as remorse.

'And then you killed her'.

'But she'd come into my personal space. She'd invaded it'.

'She'd found you out'.

'And that meant that she had to go'.

'You let her go through the trauma of the police thinking she was the murderer of James Clifton'.

'And I was sorry for that but my loyalty was to Sophie' Andrea explained. 'I did think the world of Tina but I had to use her to take any attention away from me because we hadn't finished. Tina got in the way'.

'And did Malcolm Barnes get in the way too? Is that why you killed him?'

'That was just finishing off the job'.

'For who?'

'For Sophie' said Andrea. 'It was for Sophie'.

'And your step-mother Helen?'

'I duped her into thinking that we could work together' admitted Andrea. 'It was always my intention to kill her when I got the chance. She and my father deserved to die'.

'The psychiatrist is convinced your daughter is telling the truth, Mr. Curzon' said Jeff who was sitting in his office with Brian Curzon. Jeff and Rebecca had swooped on the Curzon's house with a uniformed squad just in time to stop Andrea Kay from castrating her still drugged up father. Andrea had been arrested and charged with multiple murders and the judge at her initial court hearing had received psychiatric reports that led him to committing her to a psychiatric unit. Jeff had just played the tape of part of her first assessment with a psychiatrist there. Brian Curzon had been charged with having sex with an underage girl, Melanie Cartwright, and had been given bail pending his trial. 'But it looks like she'll be detained there for a very long time'.

Brian Curzon put his head in his hands. 'I don't know how to take all of this in, detective. I mean, watching my daughter on that tape and listening to her confess to the murder of six people including my wife'. He shook his head. 'It really is too much'.

'Your wife Helen was prepared to let your daughter kill you' Jeff reminded him. 'How does that make you feel?'

'It's beyond words, detective' said Brian. 'I admit that I've always been the kind of man who's never been satisfied with just one woman. But now I've had one wife who committed suicide over it and another who was using my own daughter to kill me. It doesn't say much for me as a man, does it'.

'You're not the first man who couldn't keep it in his trousers despite wearing a wedding ring'.

'But there aren't many men like me who seem to have poisoned the minds of so many women in his life who should've meant everything to him' said Brian. 'I mean, when Andrea went to live with her grandmother I was angry with her. She'd been so nasty and vicious to Helen. I know she was still grieving over her mother and that I was partly to blame for that because I'd left her but Andrea made no effort at all with Helen'.

'She was only a child' said Jeff. 'She must've been very confused and she needed protection from her father'.

'Yes, I know that but … look, I did my best to explain to Andrea that I was leaving her mother but that I'd always be there for her, my darling daughter. But it wasn't enough. She didn't speak to me or have any contact with me for years and I admit that I made no attempt to heal the rift that had opened up between us. I thought that when she grew up she might come to her senses and get in touch. But now it seems she never stopped being angry with me and even went way, way beyond that'.

'Well I don't think it takes an expert in these matters to see that Andrea fell under the spell of Sophie Cooper and Clarissa Dalton-Wood very easily' said Jeff who didn't want to let Curzon off the hook. He'd let his daughter down and therefore failed as a parent in the most spectacular and horrifying fashion. 'It was alright being friends with Melanie Cartwright but Melanie wasn't one of the cool gang either so Andrea must've leapt at the chance to be in league with the two newcomers who seemed so sophisticated compared with all the others. They weren't just cool. They were beyond even that. It would've given Andrea a kind of kudos with the other kids that would've put an end to all the bullying she'd gone through'.

'And I should've been there for her then too' said Brian. 'I assume from the way you talk that you're a parent?'

'Yes' said Jeff. 'I have a five year-old son'.

'Well I'll be reproaching myself the rest of my life for what I've failed to do for my daughter. I've been a useless father, detective. I've been a useless man too. And it's too late to change any of it'.

'Just one question for you, Mr. Curzon?'.

'Yes?'

'What are you going to do now about the hotel?'

'Sell it I suppose. I hadn't really thought about it'.

'And what about Bernie Connelly?'

'What about him?'

'We know you were in business with him, Mr. Curzon' said Jeff. 'So why don't you tell me all about that?'

Jonathan Freeman was surprised to see Rebecca Stockton when he answered the door.

'Are you going to let me in?' she asked.

Jonathan stood back to let Rebecca through before closing the door again. 'So what do you want?'

'You know what I want'.

'Well I presume it's not what you used to come here for'.

'Withdraw the accusations you've made against Ollie Wright'.

Jonathan leaned back against the wall of his living room and folded his arms. 'Sorry but no can do'.

'You're a liar'.

'I'm telling the truth'.

'Jonathan, you lie like a cheap fucking carpet'.

'Well you'd know all about being cheap seeing as you were in my bed without a second invitation'.

Rebecca slapped his face.

'You get that one for free but don't expect me not to fight back if you try it again'.

'Withdraw the accusation, Jonathan'.

'Why should I?'

'Because we both know it's not true'.

'Do we?'

'Don't try and be clever'.

'You never complained about that before. You said it made a change to be in bed with a man who could show some imagination'.

'Yes, well that was then and now the thought of having sex with you makes my bloody skin crawl'.

Jonathan laughed. 'Oh how we go out of our way to protect the poor little black boy who never told any of you that he was a shirt lifter'.

'Ollie Wright has a right to privacy, Jonathan. It wasn't your right to take that away from him'.

'Look, my people know what it's like to be victimized'.

'So you victimize someone else before they've had a chance to victimize you, is that it?'

'More or less, yes' Jonathan confirmed. 'You have no idea of the level of anti-Semitism out there'.

'But by falsely accusing someone of it then you're devaluing all the genuine cases. Can't you see that? I mean, what did you hope to achieve because all that's happened is that you've turned everyone in the squad against you'.

'Welcome to the world of the Jew'.

'Oh spare me! You picked on Ollie because he was black and he was gay and that makes you no better than any anti-Semite'.

'I'm the victim of anti-Semitism every single day'.

'Maybe you are' said Rebecca. 'Or maybe that's just how you like to interpret any negative action against you. I mean, am I being anti-Semitic now just by arguing with you?

Just because I disagree with you does that make me anti-Semitic in your twisted view? Should I condemn anybody who disagrees with me as sexist or on a crusade against Christians? Yes, there is anti-Semitism out there. And it's vile and it's pernicious. But what we're talking about here is not anti-Semitism. What we're talking about here is you being a complete arsehole'.

Jonathan turned his face away.

'You're the bully here, Jonathan. Ollie is completely innocent. You know it and so do I. Now I'm asking you to do the right thing'.

FIREFLIES TWENTY-ONE

Jeff wanted to confront Bernie Connelly on his own. He drove out to Connelly's house in Knutsford, Cheshire where Connelly greeted him from behind his large oak desk in his office.

'Detective Superintendent Jeff Barton' he said warmly and with an offer of his large hand. 'As I live and breathe, which incidentally I'm still doing. Much to your chagrin I expect'.

'It's not death I'm interested in when it comes to you, Connelly' said Jeff who had no intention of shaking Connelly's hand. 'It's justice'.

'And how are you going with that? Sorry your little raid the other day didn't come up with anything. It did rather prove though that I'm operating a legitimate business operation here. Of course I could've sued for police harassment but I thought no, be generous. DS Barton is still a grieving widower. I don't want to add to his troubles'.

'Don't even think of mentioning my wife's name' said Jeff, his hackles rising.

'Yes, it's still painful, I get that'.

Jeff placed the palms of his hands on Connelly's desk and leaned forward. 'Let's talk about your so-called legitimate business operation. Because that's the biggest piece of fiction there is. We've rounded up your associates in the hotel trade including Brian Curzon. You used them all to further the biggest prostitution ring in the city'.

'What can I say? It's the oldest profession in the world. Somebody is always making money out of it somewhere. I wish I'd have thought about doing it. I admire whoever did'.

'Fucking damn you Connelly! We've arrested nine men and women all of whom either owned or managed a hotel in various locations across Manchester. They all paid a percentage of their earnings to you. We know that but we didn't get it from them, not even Curzon would tell us that little nugget. None of them would name you because they were too scared. We got it from other sources'.

'A certain newspaper journalist?'

Jeff continued to stare at Connelly. 'Sharon Bellfield is still in hospital and will remain there for some time after being beaten up by your thugs. They left her for dead but luckily someone saw her lying there in that alley and called for help. Someone who was a decent human being, Connelly. Someone who therefore you wouldn't recognise'.

'Oh such harsh words, detective' said Connelly. He sat back in his high backed chair and dragged again on his cigar. 'That Sharon Bellfield is quite a character. She could drink any man under the table, that's for sure. A very tenacious young lady and no mistake. I am sorry to hear of her misfortune though. So sad to see what happens to vulnerable young women on our streets late at night. And you think I had something to do with it?'

'You were in business with the Curzon's. Helen Curzon told it all to Sharon Bellfield. But you had your people watching. You don't like the press sniffing round your business interests. That's why you had Sharon Bellfield beaten to within an inch of her life. You wanted to scare her into not going into print with what she'd found out'.

'An interesting theory. But the reality is that you can't make it stick'.

'Is that right?'

'You know I'm right, detective, just like you've always known'.

'I'll get people back from the other side of the world if I have to, Connelly'.

'Yes, yes, I know it was Anita Patel who blabbed to Miss Bellfield in the middle of a fit of conscience over her affair with the married Brian Curzon. Full marks to him for being able to pull a lovely young girl like Anita at his age, by the way. But do you really think she would come all the way back from India where she's safe in the arms of her family to testify against me in a city where she knows she wouldn't be safe anymore? Come on, detective, I think you may be losing the plot. Anyway, let's change the subject. How's Andy Kirkpatrick's wife? Has she met someone else and moved on with her life?'

'She is none of your damn business!'

'I was only asking a question out of natural human concern' said Connelly. He could see how much he was rattling Jeff and he was enjoying it. 'You see, that's another damning indictment of today's society. People are always thinking you've got an ulterior motive for showing that you care for your fellow men and women. I find that sad. Don't you find it sad, detective?'

Jeff had never wanted to kill someone as much as he wanted to kill Connelly right at that moment. 'One day I will get you for the murder of Andy Kirkpatrick, Connelly. You can bet your sordid little life on it'.

'Really? This sounds more like a vendetta than a quest for justice, detective'.

'Don't try and twist it, Connelly'.

Bernie Connelly expanded his arms out. 'Why do you think so badly of me?'

'You've got the nerve to ask me that question?'

'It's a fair question as far as I'm concerned'.

'And one of these days someone is going to ask you certain questions and you won't be able to hide the answers anymore' said Jeff. 'One day, Connelly'.

'Well I hope you're a patient man because you'll have a very long wait, detective' said Connelly, grinning like the proverbial cat who'd got the cream. 'Now if you don't mind, illuminating as this conversation is I do have things to get on with so would you like to let yourself out?'

'I concede defeat this time, Connelly. But even a cat only has nine lives and you're chalking them up rapidly'.

'A very amusing analogy' said Connelly. 'Have a nice day, detective'.

'Chief Superintendent Chambers is still off sick' said Jeff who nevertheless had to produce a report on his most recent investigation for the elected crime commissioners examination of procedures within the force. Although with Chambers off sick it had removed the immediate urgency. 'So I have the pleasure of telling you, Ollie, that Jonathan Freeman has dropped all charges against you'.

Ollie slumped in his chair and breathed out a massive sigh of relief. It took a moment or two to steady his breathing.

Jeff smiled. 'I thought you'd be pleased'.

'I'm just glad it's all over, sir'.

'You and me both, Ollie' said Jeff. 'You're a bloody good police officer and I'm proud to have you on my team. I never believed for one moment that any of this was true, Ollie'.

'Thank you, sir. I appreciate that'.

'Jonathan Freeman has made a full retraction' Jeff revealed. 'And I will make sure that this does not have any bearing on your future career'.

'None of us really knew Freeman, sir'.

'I know, Ollie, I know' said Jeff. 'And I'm sorry I brought him into the squad'.

'You weren't to know'.

'And Ollie, next time we all have a get together bring your partner. It would be good to meet him'.

Ollie smiled. 'I will do, sir. Gladly'.

'If it takes my entire career I'll get Connelly' said Jeff who was sitting with Rebecca in the pub down the road from the station. He was working his way through a pint of Guinness and Rebecca was on her second glass of white wine. 'He sits there knowing that he virtually runs this city through all the fronts for his real activities. That's something that simply cannot carry on'.

'He's bound to trip up sometime' said Rebecca. 'He slipped through your fingers this time but he won't forever, Jeff'.

'Well we'll see' said Jeff. 'You know, when I went to see him he didn't even mention the fact that his sister was in custody. He must've just washed his hands of her'.

'They're a pretty dysfunctional family' said Rebecca. 'But then look at the Curzon's. They must be one of the most dysfunctional families of them all'.

'Yes, and I don't think we got even close to seeing the full characters of Sophie Cooper and Clarissa Dalton-Wood' said Jeff as he looked into the dark Irish liquid in his glass. 'They effectively took Andrea Kay over. They truly are an evil pair of manipulators'.

'I can't help feeling a bit sorry for Andrea Kay' said Rebecca. 'I know she killed all those people but talk about being screwed up. Losing her mother so tragically and then watching her father go off with a woman who clearly didn't want Andrea around'.

'Some would say she should've just got over it and got on with her life'.

'And there's a certain amount of truth in that but it clearly wasn't that easy for her' said Rebecca. 'All the hurt and the pain twisted everything in her head'.

'I'm glad she never found out about Melanie Cartwright's baby' said Jeff. 'Or else she'd have been on her killing list'.

'Brian Curzon will go down for that'.

'Oh I'm sure he will' said Jeff. 'And good fucking riddance to the stupid, weak bastard'.

'I hear the airline have given Melanie Cartwright a warning instead of sacking her?'

'Yes, under the circumstances and all that' said Jeff. 'They decided to be lenient with her. Seamus says she's off sick with stress at the moment though. Can't say I'm surprised. She'll have the court case coming up with Brian Curzon to go through as well as those involving Cooper and Dalton-Wood'.

'How did you work out that it was Helen Curzon who helped Andrea Kay?'

'It seemed to me that it was too obvious for it to be Brian Curzon' said Jeff. 'And because of his affair with Anita Patel he became the common enemy of both Andrea and her step-mother. His murder was then the ultimate aim of them both. That's when I knew it had to be Helen Curzon'.

'And then there's poor old Tina Webb' said Rebecca. 'She was an innocent who got caught up in it all'.

'I feel like we let her down'.

'No we didn't, Jeff' said Rebecca. 'All the evidence pointed to her being the killer of James Clifton. It was only as the case went on that we were able to say for certain that she wasn't'.

'I'm going to make so damn sure that Toby knows all about what bullying is and what its long term effects can be' said Jeff. 'Andrea Kay was bullied all the way through school until Cooper and Dalton-Wood came along and replaced that with a different and altogether more sinister kind of manipulation'.

'And Jonathan Freeman used the tragic history of the Jewish people to bully Ollie Wright just because Ollie is black and gay. The bullied became the bully. Strike at them before they get a chance to strike at you'.

'That's called paranoia' said Jeff. 'It's pretty twisted too'.

'You're right there'.

'How did you get him to withdraw the allegations against Ollie?'

'I confronted him' said Rebecca. 'Told him some home truths'.

'It worked'.

'Yes it did'.

'Thank you'.

'You're welcome'.

'He wasn't worthy of you, Becky'.

Rebecca ran a hand through her hair and finished off her glass of white wine. 'That's the trouble with my life at the moment, Jeff. I don't know if I'm worthy enough for the one I want. I don't know if I ever will be'.

'That sounds like you know who the one you want is?'

'I do' said Rebecca. 'But I'm waiting for him to wake up to it'.

.

THE END

But Detective Superintendent Jeff Barton will be back soon in 'STORMS'.

STORMS PROLOGUE

Leroy tried to struggle against the restraints. He was sitting at one end of what felt like some kind of bench. There was a straight metal pole against his back and a thick metal collar round his neck that prevented him from lowering his head. Something was touching the back of his neck. He couldn't figure out what it was but it also felt like metal of some kind. His arms had been pushed back and his wrists cuffed tightly to the metal pole although his hands had been forced too far apart to be able to touch and that was causing excruciating pain in his shoulders. His knees were bent and his ankles chained to something behind him. He'd been stripped naked and he was cold. He was really cold. Tape had been placed over his mouth and eyes.

Then the man's voice filled him once more with fear.

'You may as well save your strength' said the man. 'You're really going to need it'.

Leroy heard the man step closer and then he lit a cigarette. 'You may as well face up to it, Leroy. You won't be getting out of here alive. You've come here to die my friend. Or rather you've come here for me to execute you. That's when the fun will start. Well it will for me anyway but for you it might not be so much fun. More like the unbearable torments of hell. You think you control the streets. You think you can take whatever you want and give absolutely nothing back. Well let me tell you, Leroy, it isn't going to happen anymore because I'm going to pick you all off one by one and teach the Gorton boys a valuable lesson in an eye for an eye'.

The man paused whilst he took a drag on his cigarette. Leroy was breathing rapidly and was totally consumed with terror. He didn't recognize the voice of the man but he sounded like he was probably white.

'Do you know what, Leroy? I was so keen to get down here and fill you in on what's going to be happening during your last hours on earth that I forgot to bring an ashtray. Still there are always other places to stub your fag out'.

The man grabbed Leroy's penis, pulled back the foreskin and stubbed his cigarette out on the end. He kept it there grinding the hot tobacco into the sensitive flesh. Leroy struggled once more in his restrained position. He was desperate to get away from the onslaught of sudden pain and could feel himself crying. He tried to scream but the tape across his mouth muffled the sound.

'Try and get some sleep now, there's a good boy' said the man. 'You'll need some rest whilst you contemplate your last night here on this earth'.

Leroy was hungry but the need for food and especially water was being savagely repressed by the pain that felt like it was tearing his muscles apart. He'd barely been able to sleep but when his body had given in to the need for some kind of close down he'd immediately woken up again with a start and started crying when he remembered the situation he was in.

It was true that he'd been a pretty bad boy in his time. But the Gorton boys had been his crew. More than that they'd been his family and they'd been his future. Everyone had expected him to fail at school. And he had failed. So he'd taken up arms against that same system that had predicted and orchestrated his failure. He'd beaten people up. He'd beaten up young children who'd disrespected the laws of the Gorton boys. He'd answered his mother back. He'd answered his grandparents back. He'd never told his mother just where or how he made his money. But he'd give anything to be able to tell her now.

Every time he tried to move, even a slight movement of his arms or legs, his body almost seized up with pain. He'd pissed himself. He'd had to. He'd had no choice. He could smell the pool of urine on the floor below him. It was stone cold wherever he was and yet he'd been sweating. It felt as if his legs would snap away from the rest of his body at any moment. His shoulders felt like they were on fire as they struggled to keep his arms fixed in their sockets.

He heard the door open and his body almost went into spasm with fear.

'So how was your night?' asked the man. It was the same voice as before. 'Sorry. That really was a silly question. I'll shut up and get on with preparing your painful means of death'.

Leroy heard the man walk behind him. Oh Christ what was he going to do to him? He couldn't help pissing himself again.

'Oh the waterworks' said the man. 'Still, I can't say I blame you. You must be terrified. Well you should be because this is really going to hurt'.

Leroy started crying. He could feel the tears roll down from underneath the thick tape across his eyes and across his cheeks.

'Oh' said the man. 'I suppose you want your Mum now, don't you? Well don't worry. You see I'm filming this whole thing and I'll be sending a copy of the DVD to your dear, sweet Mummy. The DVD won't show me of course. I pause the camera when I come into the room. Now, in the best traditions of all executioners I'm now going to let you have your final words'.

The man walked up and ripped the tape from Leroy's mouth. Leroy let out a loud scream and was finding it difficult to breathe.

'It's a good job nobody can hear you' said the man. 'Now, what do you want to say?'

'Please, man … please don't do this. I'll do anything … '

'Did you give any of your victims the right to a final few words? I don't suppose you did'.

'I'm … I'm sorry'

'Oh sorry is a bit late, my friend'.

'Why are you doing this to me?'

'Because you and the rest of the Gorton boys have got away with too much for too long'.

'I'm begging you, man'.

'Oh this is getting boring!' said the man who then taped Leroy's mouth up again. He watched Leroy try to struggle and got great satisfaction from seeing him twist and contort with frustration and terror.

Leroy heard some kind of mechanism twisting behind him and then the cold metal he'd been feeling against the back of his neck began to move forward and force his neck up against the metal collar. He flinched. He was finding it difficult to breathe.

'Do you know what a garotte is, Leroy? Well you're strapped to one right now. I turn the wheel at the back here and you can feel there isn't much room for maneuver so it'll take about four or five twists for it to break your neck. Then you'll be dead. Each twist will increase the pain you feel and you'll struggle more and more to breathe. Goodbye Leroy. You could've had a truly meaningful life but as it turns out your life was pretty pointless really.

Better luck next time. Now here's the second twist and with it you're just that little bit closer to death'.

Printed in Great Britain
by Amazon